Dear Miss Maitheson

Tim Heath

First published by Endeavour Media Ltd in 2018.

For
AYVIANNA SNOW
with my heartfelt thanks

Table of Contents

PROLOGUE

April 1890

The figure in the fog ... had it stopped?

'Mind where you're going, ma'am.' A man bumped into the mass of tulle and brocade and had to step to one side to proceed along the footbridge. He had been walking very slowly, though. Visibility was so poor and the tarmac walkway was so slippery that to try and hurry would have been hazardous. Only the height and solidity of the railings on either side gave any reassurance that a pedestrian would never fall into the unseen waters thirty feet below.

Because it was late and it was such a foul night, very few people were abroad. The careful clopping of carriage horses down on the Embankment could occasionally be heard. A steam tug's horn sounded regularly as the thrashing monster dragged its cargo downriver, confident that no pleasure boats would get in its way. Just as Big Ben sounded a quarter to midnight, one of the last trains out of Charing Cross banged and clattered alongside, a seemingly endless parade of ghostly carriages just visible through the gigantic girders of Hungerford Bridge. Clangs and squeals accompanied the magic lantern show of various passengers: finely dressed opera-goers returning to their mansions in Chislehurst; groups of red-faced clerks heading home after an evening in the halls of Leicester Square; dancers and waiters dozing in the third class compartments, longing for their lodgings in Hither Green.

The whole world seemed suddenly silent and very dark once the train had gone by. The clammy air soaked up light and sound and soaked the skin. You would have to have been standing right beside the stationary person on the bridge to have heard the grunts of exertion as it heaved itself up on to the rail and over.

There was a plunging splash as the body struck the water, a noise drowned out entirely by the simultaneous blast of a foghorn nearby.

1

December 2nd, 1890

Dear Miss Maitheson,

May I, through the always trustworthy columns of The Gentlewoman, *recommend to your readers an invaluable aid to finding one's way around the metropolis? Modern London has become so vast and teeming with new edifices being erected every day, it seems, that it is only too easy to lose one's way in the fog. Not everyone has the means to hire a hansom or even to take the Underground Railway and walking can be the only resource – and sometimes it is quicker.*

The patent Waterproof Guide to London Streets, *price ½d, is indestructible and completely resistant to the depredations of rain and moisture. My own has even proved useful as a makeshift umbrella. When one thinks of the number of women who, we read, disappear without trace in the city, I cannot help feeling that these unfortunate souls may well have lost their way and stumbled into the Thames or mistakenly entered some den of iniquity such as the notorious "Turkish Baths for Gentlemen" off Northumberland Avenue. I hereby rally these lost ladies with the exhortation "Seek the True Path". With the* Waterproof Guide *they shall surely find it.*

I am yours sincerely,
The Hon. Evangeline Fairfax.

No, I thought, it couldn't be published. It was too long and obviously a commercial promotion masquerading as advice. My employer, Lady Outhwaite, had laid down very clear guidelines as to what was suitable in the "Letters" page of the magazine and that included anything that might deprive the company of advertisement revenue. The following was more acceptable:

December 2nd, 1890

Dear Miss Maitheson,

Is it really true that the newly opened City and South Underground Railway has one category of carriage only for all classes of Society? If so, would you advise that ladies travel in such conditions?

Yours in bewilderment,

Mrs Duncan Reaudeene.

I wrote back:

December 5th, 1890

Dear Madam,

We recommend that you never travel unaccompanied by this means of transport, but only with a gentleman companion.

Yours faithfully,

Miss Maitheson.

The next envelope from my mailbag was made of stiff, expensive paper. A crest that I thought I recognised was embossed on the flap.

December 2nd, 1890

Dear Miss Maitheson,

I hope it is seemly so to address you. We have had no word from you since you left us in April and it was only at a recent meeting of The Maidens of Mercy that Lady Outhwaite made mention of your having joined the staff of The Gentlewoman. *Having no idea of your whereabouts I decided to write to you at the offices of the magazine. Needless to say, I do not expect this letter to appear in its pages.*

Mr Manverham and I have been staying with my brother in Edinburgh and we return to Rockbridge tomorrow to spend Christmas there with the children. You can imagine how much you have been missed and how we all think of you, especially at this time of year. We all remember fondly the carol concert that you and the servants gave in the Great Hall last December. All the family hope that you are well and completely settled.

You may perhaps welcome a little news of us, as we certainly would of you. Firstly, the children have all been in good health. James continues to enjoy school at Hans House and reads as much as ever. He has now begun on Oliver Twist. *Georgina appears to be taking after her father and has begun to display an alarming interest in mathematics. Perhaps she will become the next Miss Burdett-Coutts. And Cedric grows even more energetic and hearty. The other day, by kicking a football, he shattered the window of my sitting-room.*

There have been, as you especially will understand, a number of little changes to our way of life following the spring fiasco at Manverham's Bank. We have had to sell a number of farms and other properties on the Rockbridge estate. My brother, whose outgoings were more extravagant than ours, was obliged to sell his entire estate near Selkirk, his yacht and his private train. Thankfully we were able to retain all our staff. Lord Moffat had to dismiss a large number and there was no pension or cottage for Miss Jardine, either. I can't imagine where old "Nanny Selkirk" is now if she hasn't drunk herself to death.

I should tell you that James wanted to write to you himself, but we dissuaded him on the grounds of not knowing your address. Perhaps such a correspondence should wait until he is a little older and has seen more of the world.

We all send our warmest good wishes for Christmas and for 1891 and trust we shall hear from you before long.

Yours ever,

Eleanor Manverham.

Oh, the memories of Rockbridge Hall that this letter prompted. It really was time I got in touch with Lady Eleanor. After all, she had been my benefactor for so long. It was foolish of me to pretend that I had no past, but when would I have a future?

The present intruded into my reverie in the form of Mrs Jones, Lady Outhwaite's whipping boy and general slave. She was small and timid and dressed in the manner of an elderly spinster although she was known to have a husband in what Lady Outhwaite described as "the wilds of Wandsworth". She had been helped by The Maidens of Mercy, who assisted women who had fallen on hard times. Lady Outhwaite was its President. It was rumoured that Mrs Jones originated from the slums of Swansea but had been brought up by a family in Middlesbrough before being rescued by the Maidens and given a job as a scullery maid at Outhwaite Towers. Her attempt at gentility was pathetic and she knew it, but anything less would not serve in the surroundings of serene grandeur that was Lady Outhwaite's world. Self-conscious about her extraordinary accent, Mrs Jones spoke little. On this occasion it was merely to say: 'Her ladyship would like to see you in the Boardroom, Mr Maitheson'.

2

It was always a tonic to hear myself addressed correctly. The title of "Miss" had been insisted upon for the "Letters" page by my employer. Without question, she maintained, ladies preferred to divulge their problems and questions on etiquette to a member of their own sex. There had been no other vacancies available at the magazine when I approached them. My reference from Eleanor Manverham had certainly helped me secure the position and I had been given a three-month trial at a very low salary on condition that I suppressed my masculinity on the page. In this I had been successful. Whenever a reader's letter taxed my knowledge of Society mores I would consult the various published guides, review copies of which were stored in the office library. If still at a loss I would flatter the divers debutantes and dowagers who worked at *The Gentlewoman* by appealing to their superior knowledge, which they loved to flaunt for a mere man who was their social inferior. Heaven forbid that these were paid employees. They were far too grand to admit to actually working. They served Society and saw their assistance to the journal as a charitable contribution to the well-being of the Empire. Their proprietor looked down on wages and so did they.

Very seldom had I put a foot wrong. Lady Outhwaite examined every syllable with a gimlet eye and I would be informed at once of any error. Advertisements, illustrations, text, page layout – everything was scrutinised through her lorgnette before being sanctioned for publication. There was an "editor", a gentleman called Mr Wilkins, but he was a puppet whose main purpose was to control matters in the press rooms in the basement. Lady Outhwaite considered this a male preserve of sweat, noise and fumes. Mr Wilkins was the chief engineer of the ship, while her ladyship was the captain, owner and figurehead.

Margarita Outhwaite (*née* Slabb) had begun her career as a village school teacher "somewhere in Lancashire", as she put it. She had been diligent and frugal and had set her cap at the most ambitious young man she could find. This was an apprentice engineer called Reginald Outhwaite. After they had married they had enhanced their position in the community by doing charity work and performing with music societies. Margarita was a keen but dreadful singer. She founded a ladies' choir which she ruled with a rod of iron. One of her earliest triumphs had been to secure the composer Arthur Sullivan as its Patron. Meanwhile Reginald had opened a small factory making rivets, a business run ruthlessly and aggressively which had expanded over the years with the burgeoning of the railways. By 1880 Sir Reginald, as he had become, was one of the Empire's leading industrialists. There were very few iron bridges in the world that were not held together by his patent bolts. As he bored listeners with accounts of how many thousands of his invention had been supplied for the building of Tower Bridge he would make his favourite joke: 'Riveting stuff, eh, riveting stuff!'

His wife in the meantime had studied social refinement and elocution assiduously. Her philanthropy gave her a leg up to ever higher rungs of Society. She considered that she had arrived when she was made a Lady-in-Waiting to the elderly Queen at Windsor, which was not far from Outhwaite Towers. From such pinnacles Lady Outhwaite wielded great power and dropped great names. Her founding of *The Gentlewoman* increased her influence. Its Boardroom on the first floor of the offices in Bedford Street was, in fact, a throne room.

'You are one minute late, Mr Maitheson,' said her ladyship imperiously as I entered the chamber to see her seated at the end of the long table. Next to her stood Mrs Jones. Along either side sat the cohorts of Society ladies who were in charge of the various pages. Mr Wilkins, the only other man in the room, sat humbly next to a console table on which stood the speaking trumpet apparatus that communicated with his office in the basement. 'We must be ahead of the times, not behind them, Mr Maitheson,' her ladyship continued. 'To be a second late is unfortunate, to be a minute late is social death.'

I nodded meekly and sat down. When I could next steal a glance at my employer I was able to take in her gown of purple and black silk trimmed with fur, the intricate lace blouse on the bosom of which rested her gold lorgnette on its chain and the enormous hat surmounted with ostrich feathers. Her face, a mask of serene complacency, was dominated by large brown eyes that stared like those of an owl.

Mrs Jones had handed Lady Outhwaite the agenda for the meeting. Nothing was for discussion. Pens and pencils hovered anxiously as her ladyship spoke: 'Mr Wilkins, I trust your pen is poised. There will be a number of amendments to the current edition. Where are we? Tuesday. They will have to be in place by the end of today. Ladies and gentlemen, please forgive my rushing through. I am expected for lunch at Windsor and Sir Reginald's train is being held for me at Waterloo. Jones, please see that the carriage is outside in ten minutes. Now, the first item is in "Reports on Weddings" where I see that one of the bridegrooms is called Mr Albert Hall. Caroline, are you sure that is correct? You are sure? Very well. Mr Wilkins, please insert a "(*sic*)" after the gentleman's name. Our reputation for truth and accuracy may otherwise be threatened. So. Augusta dear, it pains me to criticise your Christmas poem, but this is worse than the worst of Wordsworth. Allow me to read it out:

"Pensées de Noël

Hark the choirs of angels singing;
List to country church bells ringing;
See the lambs to mothers clinging.

Hushed the snowflakes falling, falling;
Hear the shepherds calling, calling;
'Tend the Infant bawling, bawling."

'It's not your *chef d'oeuvre*, is it, Augusta? Why don't you try something else for next week? Remove the poem, Mr Wilkins. Which brings me to the Carol Concert which, as you all should know, is in two weeks' time on December 19th. I am pleased to report that a large number of tickets have been taken, but St. Paul's Church is larger than it appears from the outside. As with last year, Father Grantley is donating the proceeds to The Maidens of Mercy. So will you all please try your utmost to sell another hundred tickets? Sadly, our Patron Eleanor Manverham will be in Nottinghamshire, but she is generously providing all the food and wine. After much hesitation I have agreed to sing an aria from *The Messiah*. Mr Maitheson, will you accompany me? I gather your musical talents are hidden under a bushel. Thank you. Perhaps you would be good enough to collect the music from the vicar later today. He is expecting you at five o'clock. Finally, we have received a wire from *The Gentlewoman* in Dublin. An infernal machine has exploded in the Post Office killing two horses and a driver. Adriana, I believe you know Colonel Ford of Her Majesty's

Inspectorate of Explosives. He will grant you an interview at noon today at the Charing Cross Hotel. We will need your copy by six o'clock. Mr Wilkins, please ensure space is left for three hundred words in the "News" section. As I said earlier, we must be ahead of the times … and any other journal of note. Ah, Jones! The carriage is waiting, I take it. Tick, tock, "we must obey the time…".'

3

Five 'o clock was chiming from the gallery of St. Paul's as I entered the nave. I had just come through the double doors from the vestibule when I noticed a movement in the far corner to my left, just beyond the pulpit.

'Hello?' I called into the gloom. 'Father Grantley?' Silence and stillness. Now that my eyes had accustomed themselves a little to the candle-lit interior I was able once again to admire Inigo Jones' elegant, airy space – more like an assembly room than a church. There was style but not extravagance in the design, in keeping with the orders of Covent Garden's principal landlord the Earl of Bedford. It was a perfect setting for Handel's *The Messiah*, a section of which was to be given in the Carol Concert. I had learned from Mrs Jones during the afternoon in the office that Lady Outhwaite's solo was to be the final number in an excerpt which would also involve a chorus, a chamber orchestra and two other soloists from the Royal Italian Opera. My employer had been concerned that the band would drown her out, which was why she had asked for a piano accompaniment.

'She asked you because no one else would play for her. They're all too scared,' Mrs Jones had confided. 'And no professional would go near her.'

'Well, I'm also scared of her,' I had whispered back. 'It's just that I can't afford to lose my position. The others, who are pianists, don't have to earn a living.'

'You'll look lovely in evening dress,' Mrs Jones had simpered. 'Oh, to be twenty-five again! Pretty as a picture, you'll be.'

There it was again behind the pulpit, a quick rustling noise near the floor. 'Father Grantley?' I called a second time.

'Oh there you are.' The voice came from behind me. 'Mr Maitheson is it? I didn't hear you come in and came to look for you. I'm afraid I was somewhat absorbed in my hobby.' Through the double doors had entered a plump clergyman with the demeanour of Mr Pickwick but with more hair than that beloved gentleman. A beaming smile welcomed me from under his half-moon spectacles. 'How do you do? I'm Giles Grantley. Come into the vestry and we'll have some tea.'

'Mr Grantley, is there someone lurking over there in the corner?'

'Probably just one of my tramps. We allow them in during the day in winter and move them on when we lock up.'

A set of steps up from the vestibule led into a large vestry with comfortable-looking sofas either side of a good fire. A long table under the window was brightly lit by two lamps and there, spread out in the pools of light, was the vicar's hobby: the table's surface was a twinkling, gleaming sea of coils, cog wheels, springs and tiny brass screws lapping around a mahogany clock case.

'Some of the parishioners can't afford to send their timepieces away for repair so I help them out and in return I can sometimes call on them for help around the church – lifting and decorating and so on. Come and sit down.'

When we were settled with cups of tea I felt a wonderful sense of calm in that cosy room. The thick walls of the church entirely blotted out the noise of Covent Garden. Oases of quiet were hard to come by in London. A comforting sense of safety and reassurance was also in short supply unless you belonged to the wealthier classes.

Mr Grantley was looking through a portfolio of music and took out some pages. 'Margarita would insist on singing the most difficult aria she could find. Here it is, *I know that my redeemer liveth*. Beautiful, but interminable. By the time she's finished singing it the audience will be wondering if their Redeemer is living or dying,' the vicar chuckled slyly. 'Have you been with *The Gentlewoman* long?'

'Oh no,' I replied. 'Only since October. My trial period is nearly at an end and I'm hoping to be kept on.'

'Do you know Adriana Creston?'

I replied that the Hon. Adriana was one of Lady Outhwaite's favourites and had been the correspondent dispatched to interview Colonel Ford at the Charing Cross Hotel.

'Goodness, how interesting,' Grantley exclaimed. 'These modern girls … An atrocity in Dublin, you say? Doubtless the work of the Fenians. I hear about the struggle for Home Rule all the time from some of my flock. So many of the desperate poor round here come from Ireland. Some of them attend Corpus Christi, of course. I meet them in the hostels off Drury Lane or in Seven Dials. It's all very sad. The whole world comes to London, it seems, and trying to help everyone is like trying to turn back the tide. Oh no—'

A knock at the vestry door seemed to signify another call on the vicar's kindness when a deep Italianate bass voice called out: 'Signor Grantley? May I come in? It's signor Baritoni from the Opera House,' and into the room came an enormous gentleman exquisitely dressed in immaculate evening clothes. He was bald but with jet black hair at the temples and at the back of his head. His elegantly trimmed beard and moustache also showed no signs of greying, although their owner must have been in his fifties. His blue-grey eyes were beacons of geniality and grace and his voice was extravagantly cultured and mellifluous. The vicar and I rose as introductions were made.

'Signor Baritoni, this is Richard Maitheson, Lady Outhwaite's newest recruit at *The Gentlewoman*. Mr Maitheson, may I present Stuardo Baritoni, who is Augustus Harris' House Manager at the Royal Italian Opera? You are both to be contributors to Lady Outhwaite's Carol Concert. Signor Baritoni will be singing the bass solo. Such an exciting aria, it always thrills me. It's like a call to arms.' In a somewhat querulous tenor Mr Grantley suddenly broke into song: '"Why do the nations so furiously rage together, why do the people imagine a vain thing?" Stuardo will sing it better than me, of course.'

'Well, I will try, padre. I can only say how much I welcome the chance to sing anything at all. It is frustrating sometimes, working in an opera house but not being allowed to make music myself. But I never felt I was good enough to be a professional.'

Father Grantley was extracting the relevant pages of music for Baritoni as he said: 'You do honour to the Opera House in other ways, signor.'

'But signori, I have to tell you the latest news.' The House Manager was clearly bursting to make an announcement. His whole frame trembled with excitement as he said: 'We have already written to inform Lady Outhwaite: The Prince of Wales has graciously agreed to attend the gala performance in aid of The Maidens of Mercy.'

The vicar gasped in astonishment. He was obviously delighted and yet seemed to be circumspect, as if the news was too good to be true. 'Are you sure, Stuardo?'

The angel of glad tidings smiled conspiratorially as he confided: 'We have arranged the programme especially for His Royal Highness. February 12th – mark your calendars. I am sure her ladyship will give you all the details.'

Oh yes, she most certainly will, I thought to myself. Already I could foresee the conferences and consultations at the Opera House and the endless letters to and from the officials at Marlborough House. Lady Outhwaite would have a field day.

It was time to make my way home and for Signor Baritoni to return to work across the Piazza, so we all parted company full of purpose and excitement and I made my way towards Waterloo. I would walk, I thought. I would cross the river via Hungerford Bridge.

4

Sometimes, when I was roughly halfway across the Hungerford footbridge, I would pause and remember that fateful night in April.

It had been a couple of weeks after I had returned to London from Rockbridge Hall. I was still trying to find my bearings in life. The contrast between the peaceful, ordered park of the Manverhams' estate and the loud, crowded clatter of the capital had come as a shock. It had taken days before I could acknowledge how much I missed that family and the comfortable routine of life in a country house – and to think that I had imagined myself in danger there.

I had had no choice about where to go when I reached London. I had only felt able to turn to my brother Arthur who had kindly offered me shelter in his house in Battersea. I was still living there now, eight months later.

Arthur had just turned thirty. He was an army ordnance clerk at Chelsea Barracks. He and his wife Violet lived in one of those countless small terraced houses that lined the streets running down off Lavender Hill, cowering in the shadow of Battersea's ever-growing Town Hall. The hoot and puff of locomotives going in and out of Clapham Junction was pretty constant, but the proximity of that station and its convenience for central London had proved a godsend in my efforts to find work. This involved writing letters to managers daily, answering advertisements in *The Stage* and attending auditions in the West End.

Back in April I was between the main seasons for theatre work. Pantomimes had finished their runs and, very often, their auditions for the following Christmas. Spring tours were already underway and many seaside managements had already booked their artistes for the summer. There were, however, a number of little metropolitan music halls and gentlemen's clubs that needed a bespoke drag act from time to time. This was one of my specialities. Sometimes accompanying myself on the piano, I would render such ditties as *Mother doesn't love me anymore* and *I like my cream all clotted on my strawberry*. It was outside just such an establishment, The Pampered Peacock in Craven Street, that I ran into Larry again.

I had attended an interview with the club's manager. Naturally he had expected to see me in female attire, but before the place became busy, at half past ten in the evening. There was a pea souper fog that night and under cover of darkness it had been possible to travel into town in one of my lady's outfits unnoticed and unaccosted. The meeting had gone well and I'd been offered a "shop window" week of performances. My euphoria at being welcomed back into the entertainment profession was such that I had gone to a pub round the corner to treat myself to a large brandy and soda. All the fear and strain of the preceding year and a half began to slip away. I quickly downed a second brandy and soda and left the place feeling invincible. And as I passed The Pampered Peacock in the fog I literally bumped into Larry. He was about to go into the club.

He and I had been lovers whilst touring in *The Pirates of Penzance*. Some weeks after the run had finished we had lost touch. I hadn't saved much from the tour and had had to take other work, lying low and working in an East End pub until the chance had come to work in Nottinghamshire at Rockbridge Hall. I had hidden from everyone, including Larry, including my family. There had been no letters and no forwarding addresses.

He didn't recognise me at first, what with the dark, the fog and my costume. Then, when he heard my voice he looked at me more closely. He looked around furtively, then whispered:

'I thought you were dead. It is you, isn't it, Richard?'

'Yes.'

'What happened to you? I wrote and called. You disappeared.'

'I know. There wasn't anyone else. It's just I was frightened and had to hide.'

'Who from?'

'I can't tell you. Look, can we talk inside the club?'

'No, Richard, I don't think that's a good idea.'

'Why not? I'm going to be working there soon.'

'What? No, Richard, listen. I'm glad you're alive, but it's been nearly two years and things have changed for me – and London's changed too. We're all frightened, men like us, and we have to be more careful. I think it would be best if we wish each other luck and part. I've got to go in now. Please don't follow me. Take care of yourself.'

He had backed away, turned and let himself in. Then the door was closed in my face. I heard it being bolted from the inside. I wasn't standing for that. I had just been welcomed by the club, after all, so I knocked loudly. With no response I knocked again and shouted to be let in. The hurt I felt was aggravated by the drink and I had started hammering and yelling when the door was suddenly opened by the manager I had met earlier. He looked me in the eye and said sternly: 'Larry won't come out and you are not coming in. Quieten down. We pride ourselves on discretion here. You'll bring the police down on us if you don't shut up. As I said, Larry won't come out and you're not coming in and I think it would be better if I withdrew my offer of an engagement. Please don't come back. Good night.' Again the door was closed in my face.

I felt numb. I felt winded. This was something worse than rejection which, God knew, I had felt before many times. It was as if I was being told something but I couldn't make out what was being spoken. It was as if the speaker didn't care if I understood the message or not, because I didn't matter anymore, and it wasn't worth anyone's time to explain what I wouldn't understand anyway. Who *could* understand it? It was cold and uncaring like the fog and the darkness and, it seemed, the whole of London.

Seeing nothing, feeling nothing, I took slow steps down Craven Street to the Embankment, up on to the footbridge and out over the river. I remember Big Ben striking quarter to midnight and a train rumbling past. I remember feeling unable to stand the pain any longer. There was a struggle to heave myself up over the railing and the relief of feeling free at the top, of feeling free as I fell.

I had not been ready to die. If I had been I would have forced my body to keep rigid as I sank. I would have kept my mouth open and filled my lungs with water. The thwack, splash and shock woke me up. There was loud bubbling and spluttering that seemed outside of me. The river smelt disgusting and tasted foul. I was convulsed with fury, fear and choking. Thrashing panic overcame me. Then, just as I felt myself losing consciousness, the night air revived me as I came back to the surface. I couldn't call out, only splutter and vomit, but a voice from the past called out to me: 'Don't struggle. Put your head back and your arms out at the sides. Relax and float!'

All very well when you're being swept towards the sea, but it worked. It gave me time to think and then act. The boots: kick them off one by one –

gone. Already easier to swim. Tear off the wig. Unhook the upper cape – that gave my arms more freedom. These were clothes designed for quick changes in the wings. They were destined to be discarded in a hurry. No one was needed to unlace the false corset or unbutton the skirt at the back … Slip down the false petticoat … Now in just my drawers and a blouse I was free and swimming. Where? I couldn't see a thing. And then I struck a cold, slimy thing, a chain. I wrapped my arms around it. If I could cling to this slippery, icy object I might just stop myself being swept further downstream. I held on and slowly gathered my strength to shout out … again and again.

It must have been at least half an hour before I heard an answering shout and that was to tell me to keep on shouting because whoever it was needed my voice in order to navigate through the fog. Eventually a police launch loomed over me and I was hauled aboard, shivering, choking and sobbing with gratitude.

I wept too for times past, for that summer of '88 which appeared in my memory like a magic lantern show, when *The Pirates* had played Bournemouth and Larry had taught me how to swim.

5

DUBLIN POST OFFICE EXPLOSION

Following the outrage on Tuesday last, 5th December, our Correspondent interviewed 'l'homme du jour' Colonel A. Ford of Her Majesty's Inspectorate of Explosives.

Colonel Ford was pleased to see me in the recently redecorated salon of the Charing Cross Hotel, Strand, London. Foremost in my thoughts was the provenance of the new wallpaper, which I can now confirm as being from Liberty's 'Les Arts Florissants' collection. It is soothing to the eye and spirit, for which I was grateful, as troubled times were under consideration.

One was immediately reassured by the colonel's demeanour of solid calm, greatly reinforced by his suit of grey tweed (from Gieves and Hawkes, Savile Row, he told me). The gentleman is in his fifties, I should say, with an iron-grey beard through which one can discern a rather charming wry smile quite in harmony with his glittering blue eyes. His hair is closely cut, as befits a military man, and from the faint scent of his hair lotion I knew at once that Trumper's of Curzon Street was his barber. A remarkable detail that I feel I must report is the delicacy of his hands and lightness of his touch. Throughout his gracious serving of coffee there came not the faintest sound of china or silver, which the hotel manager assured me was all supplied by Thomas Goode and Company.

Knowing how valuable the colonel's time is, I confined my questioning to the one matter uppermost in the mind of every hostess, namely: given the number of incidents this year involving infernal machines, did the authorities anticipate any disruption of London Society's Winter Season. The answer was a confident 'Absolutely not.'

'Excellent, Adriana,' Lady Outhwaite purred, nodding graciously to the debutante standing opposite her in the Boardroom. The older woman was a Whistleresque vision in pearl and silver, the younger a symphony in white of Pre-Raphaelite chiffon and lace. It was well known in the office that Adriana was our employer's favourite Society beauty amongst the bevy of girls who vied for the proprietor's attention. With her honey-blonde hair and ice-blue eyes she reminded me a little of Eleanor Manverham, though she was much younger than my former benefactor.

Laid out meticulously along the table were the page proofs of the current edition. Since nine o'clock that morning Miss Creston, Mrs Jones, Mr Wilkins and I had been required to attend her ladyship's "Inspection", a weekly ritual charged with suppressed hysteria that took place every Wednesday morning. It was now half past eleven and there was more than one sigh of relief to be heard as Lady Outhwaite lowered her lorgnette and pronounced the time-honoured and longed-for command: 'Very well, Mr Wilkins, you may proceed.'

The order was immediately relayed via the editor's speaking trumpet to the subterranean press rooms. By four o'clock the entire edition would be ready to be carted away to the various centres of distribution.

'Jones,' Lady Outhwaite ordered, pointing to Adriana's article,' "The Inventory of Influence".'

One of the many duties of the downtrodden Mrs Jones was to maintain a record of any businesses, individuals or institutions that had been favourably mentioned in *The Gentlewoman*. This complete tally of editorial patronage was yet another wand of influence that Lady Outhwaite wielded without shame. There, in Mrs Jones' careful copperplate script, were the dates, names and relevant page numbers relating to every edition of the magazine that had bestowed a free advertisement or had enhanced the reputation of a public persona.

'Yes, my lady,' the drudge murmured, sagging beneath the weight of an enormous ledger. Within moments she was bending to her task.

'Thank you, Mr Wilkins, that will do for today. Miss Creston, Mr Maitheson, please follow me. When you've finished that, Jones, please bring us coffee in my office.'

*

'Why are you giggling, child?'

'I am so sorry, Lady Outhwaite,' Adriana replied. 'The tension in the Boardroom was almost unbearable. I believe I may be having a slightly hysterical reaction. It was my first Inspection.'

'And you, Mr Maitheson? Are you to have hysterics also?'

'I don't think so, my lady. I have attended the Inspection before.'

'So you have, Mr Maitheson. You have become quite a pillar of the establishment in your short time with us. May I begin by saying that I am very pleased with your work to date; "Miss Maitheson" would seem to inspire confidence in our readers and I congratulate you.'

'Thank you, my lady.'

'I believe ...' there was a pause as her ladyship consulted a large diary on the desk in front of her, '... Yes; I believe your three months' trial finishes at the end of this month. So I am pleased to inform you that I have decided to make your situation here official from the start of January. I trust your conduct until then will reward my faith in you?'

'Yes, my lady, it will. Thank you.'

'Very good. There will be an improvement in terms, of course, and an increase in salary – but not so great that you may think of marrying. Is that understood?'

'I did not have matrimony in mind, Lady Outhwaite.'

'I am pleased to hear it. Modern life is ruined by young men getting married. They are rarely in a position to afford it. I speak, of course, of the lower orders.'

'Naturally, my lady,' I replied, not greatly bothered by my employer's contumely. She was like a character in a play, "alone worth the price of admission".

'Which brings me to the reason why I invited you and Miss Creston into this humble hub of the Empire.'

Adriana looked perplexed at being bracketed with a man quite obviously out of her social sphere but she did not look at me. She only adopted an attentive smile as Lady Outhwaite turned on Mrs Jones who, once coffee had been served, had been hovering in a corner.

'Stop lurking, Jones. You're like an incubus out of a Gothic novel. Go and order the carriage for half past twelve. I am meeting Sir Reginald at the Savoy.'

'Very good, m'lady,' the unfortunate woman muttered sadly, as if she felt her place in the hierarchy of English literature only too keenly. Eagerly, but humbly, she left the room.

'Now,' Lady Outhwaite continued once the door had closed and had shut out the ever-present clatter of typewriters, 'you may have heard on the grapevine, or even read somewhere, that Sir Reginald is about to start a splendid new charitable scheme called The Sons of Toil. It is an attempt to help men who are out of work – it could be seen as the brother charity of The Maidens of Mercy. There is to be a luncheon reception for the Press at the Savoy on Monday and I want you young people to write about the event for *The Gentlewoman*. Miss Creston, you will concentrate on the hotel with a view to adorning the pages of my Inventory. And you, Mr Maitheson, are to write about the scheme itself from the point of view of men without work. After all, you had no work for months before we gave you shelter from the storm. Is that not so?'

'Indeed, my lady,' I admitted.

'There may well be letters on the subject in the next few weeks, so you should be very well placed to respond to them, writing as "Miss Maitheson" of course – but your article may be written under your proper name.'

'Really? Oh thank you, my lady – at last!'

*

'Congratulations, Mr Maitheson,' whispered Adriana as we descended the stairs to the humbler offices on the ground floor. 'If only my parents would allow me to work for money.'

'I dare say you'll have a wealthy husband soon enough, Miss Creston, and financial concerns will be gone forever.'

'Allow me to disabuse you of such common precepts, Mr Maitheson. I should like to buy you lunch at The Bedford Head. A little celebration is in order. Do you accept?'

'The Bedford Head? And without a chaperone? Buying *me* lunch? Lady Outhwaite would have you drummed out of Society.'

'That is a trauma with which I would endeavour to come to terms,' Adriana replied loftily.

*

One thing I learned in my short theatrical career is that you can't set too much store by false chivalry or false pride if you are poor. If someone, man or woman, is kind enough to offer to buy you lunch in a pub and you are having to be careful with your funds, you should accept gracefully. So I was pleased to accompany Miss Creston along Maiden Lane to The Bedford Head. It was too cold to walk much further during the hour allowed. Most of the ladies who staffed *The Gentlewoman* brought their own cold collations to the office in elegant hampers, or patronised the grand establishments along the Strand. Lady Outhwaite's "Inventory of Influence" always ensured them a good table, attentive service and favourable terms.

The Bedford Head, however, though respectable, was not genteel and usually only saw female customers at night after curtain down in the theatres. Quite a few of the printers from *The Gentlewoman* and neighbouring magazines would go there, as would Mr Wilkins and I. Debutantes were unheard of and as soon as Adriana and I entered the saloon there was a surprised silence, followed by licentiously raised eyebrows and low chuckles. A wag from the press rooms was heard to groan 'Oh God, we're going to have a poetry reading ...'

None of this fazed Miss Creston, who confidently went to the bar and ordered a bottle of Guinness for herself and a pint of bitter for me. She also asked for some ham sandwiches to be brought over to a table in a quiet corner at the back.

'Well, I'm honoured, Miss Creston. Thank you, but you won't get presented at Court carrying on like this.'

'I think I might, though. Lady Outhwaite's influence will protect me.'

'But what about appearances? She cares for those. What about the magazine's reputation? Its writers must be above reproach.'

'My father is part-owner of *The Gentlewoman* in Dublin. If he falls out with Lady Outhwaite the journal's Irish branch will close and Margarita's empire will lose a province. She can't afford to offend the Anglo-Irish aristocracy. If she did, she would lose her position at Windsor.'

I had heard in the office that Adriana's father was Lord Cormanston, the premier viscount of Ireland. That he was a major shareholder in the magazine I had not known. So Miss Creston was all right, but what about me? I had a position to think of as well.

'Do you always drink Guinness?' I asked my companion, as she eyed me thoughtfully over the creamy head of her drink. 'I find it disgusting.'

'I think if I'd ordered champagne I would have given offence.'

A plate of sandwiches, some mustard, cutlery and a couple of side plates were set before us by a woman whose demeanour suddenly made me wonder what Mrs Jones did at lunch time. She was never in the office. Perhaps she was stored in a box on the back of Lady Outhwaite's carriage ...

After we had sampled the establishment's fare, which I enjoyed even if Adriana did not, I felt bold enough to ask another question: 'How do you know Colonel Ford, Miss Creston?'

There was a careful silence on the other side of the table and I wondered if I had committed some horrendous solecism, when Adriana replied: 'Margarita can be so tactless sometimes. There was no need to tell the entire editorial crowd. Colonel Ford is a friend of Papa's. They served in the army together ages ago. Andrew – that's the Colonel – used to come and stay with us at Cormanston.'

'My, my, you are well protected and connected. I hope you will protect me from Lady Outhwaite if she hears about this little luncheon – for which I'm most grateful, by the way.'

'Oh, don't mention it. It's my pleasure. As for protecting you, I might do that … and I might not.'

6

I couldn't leave it there, just allow the words to pass unremarked upon as if I hadn't heard them or, indeed, was happy to be talked to in that way. The tone of her comment was charmingly provocative, not threatening, and her smile as she made it was teasing. It was very attractive. She expected a response but I was conscious that caution was necessary. She was, of course, unaware of the experience I had with the machinations of actors and actresses; of women who, because they were adept at manipulating children, believed they had the right to manipulate adults also. And then there was the fact that Adriana had no idea of my experience in subterfuge and of defending myself against aristocrats far wealthier than, and quite as grand as, the Cormanstons. Nevertheless, caution was necessary if I was to keep my position at *The Gentlewoman*. Adriana would certainly feel insulted if I did not rise to her challenge, however, so to buy some time I said: 'Would you care for another drink, Miss Creston?'

'Well then, I might protect you after all,' she replied coquettishly. 'Thank you.'

Whatever work Adriana was planning to do in the afternoon, if any, I had to return to the magazine's mailbag, so I bought us a half round and returned our plates to the bar. We didn't have much time left, I noticed. The enormous clock staring out from between the shelves of bottles showed nearly half past one. There was probably only time to ask a single question. On balance I calculated that it would not come as unexpected or disrespectful: 'Miss Creston, I hope you won't think me intrusive, but may I ask what ambitions you have at *The Gentlewoman*? I can't imagine you are solely interested in wallpaper.'

'How right you are, Mr Maitheson.'

She looked straight into my eyes and I couldn't look away. She was beguiling, disturbing almost. I didn't feel threatened or intimidated. I felt understood and forgiven. 'What I want,' she continued in a voice of suppressed excitement, 'is to be a published author.'

'Is that all?' I stammered. 'But you are already published, in the magazine.'

'Yes, but only anonymous articles of trivial "feminine interest". I write those just to keep Lady Outhwaite happy. You have a writing name – as a woman and very soon as a man too. Debutantes can't be seen or known to be published. So I must build up a collection of anonymous work until I can persuade an editor to give me a name. I might have to wait until I'm married!'

'What is it that you want to write?'

'Poems and novels,' she gushed. 'Romances and mysteries and tales of unbridled passion in the wilds of Australia.'

'Well, that certainly would not meet with Lady Outhwaite's approval – the Australia part, I mean.'

Adriana laughed before confiding: 'I want to replace Augusta Hantry as *The Gentlewoman*'s Poetess. Goodness knows, it shouldn't be too difficult to match her talent.'

Knowing that everyone in the office felt for Augusta and that her position was not secure, I felt safe in expressing my agreement.

It was time to bring our conversation to a close and we returned to the magazine on the corner of Bedford Street and Maiden Lane. A carriage was waiting there and for an alarming moment I thought it was Lady Outhwaite's and that she had been hoping to catch us, but Adriana explained that it was for her. Sure enough, the Cormanston crest adorned the doors.

'I have to go home to rest for a ball tonight. I shall see you again very soon, Mr Maitheson.'

'I look forward to it, Miss Creston, and thank you again for lunch.'

*

December 3rd, 1890

Dear Miss Maitheson,

My younger son, who is seven years old, has only recently made a tearful confession. Two months ago he overheard an old nursemaid in Crystal Palace Park. She was showing the dinosaur models to her young charges. This woman informed the children that the gigantic creatures were real, that they kept very still when looked at, but came to life when one's back was turned and devoured little children who had been naughty. My child was terrified and guilt-ridden and begged me to protect him. Please can you reassure him that the old nursemaid I mentioned is an evil purveyor of lies? My son's name is Nicholas.

Yours in distress,

Mrs Sebastian Beare.

December 6th, 1890

Dear Master Nicholas,
Your Mama is absolutely right to tell you that the dinosaurs in question are not real, are statues dating from the 1850s and that the old nursemaid you overheard was lying to those children. If you have been a little naughty yourself, you must not be unhappy. Your mother and father will forgive you and, I am sure, give you lovely presents at Christmas. I sincerely hope so. Please feel at liberty to show this letter to any of your friends who may also have heard this wicked rumour.
Yours sincerely,
Miss Maitheson.

I felt absolutely confident that Lady Outhwaite, who had no children of her own, would publish this correspondence. Its potential to tug at maternal heartstrings everywhere was enormous. Circulation would soar and my position at the magazine would be consolidated.

It had been a good day. I felt a shift inside myself, something pleasant but hard to identify. A loosening of my diaphragm had taken place and my chest seemed free of tension and anxiety. Could everything be all right? Could it?

No; there was a doubt. A faint memory stirred unpleasantly. To know what it was, I felt that I had to read between the lines of a mental diary, or of a letter thrown away long ago. It was as if I had glimpsed the slowly moving coils of an anaconda beneath the surface of a muddy river. Would it rear its head? And if so, when?

*

My brother's house in Battersea was solidly built and when you shut the front door the outside world disappeared. The noise of Clapham Junction, with its endless steam whistles and bustling crowds of commuters, was forgotten. The horse drawn omnibuses clattering out of the dark had been avoided; Lavender Hill had been climbed and the building works of the emerging Town Hall had been skirted: I was home.

The inner porch was warmed and scented by the kitchen at the rear of the house where my sister-in-law Violet was preparing an evening meal. I was making my way down the passage to greet her when my brother Arthur suddenly emerged from the front parlour on my right. I remembered it was Wednesday, when he only worked a half day so was home earlier than usual. The room from which he came, like most front parlours, was seldom used, so immediately I felt that something was wrong when he whispered 'Richard, old chap, could you come in here, please?'

The room was cold and oppressive. There was no fire. Already apprehensive from Arthur's headmaster-like invitation, I was made more nervous by the sight of my parents in their cabinet photographs on the mantelpiece. I was estranged from them, had been for many years since they had expressed disapproval of my theatrical profession and suspicions of my immorality. Now they seemed ready to supervise a scene of guilt and confession amongst the palms and lace curtains. The atmosphere was not enlivened either by the fact that my brother had not changed out of his uniform. Gently, he bid me sit down and then quickly closed the door. He did not sit opposite me but paced the room thoughtfully. He was taller than me and whereas I took after my mother in appearance, Arthur had my father's stern good looks, hawkish brown eyes and brilliantined black hair.

'We're going to have to be quick, Richard. Sorry to bustle you into this morgue, but I wanted to catch you without alarming Violet.'

'What's wrong?'

'Are you in trouble, old chap?'

'No.'

'Nothing to do with those people at Rockbridge Hall?'

'No. Apart from one letter yesterday, addressed to the magazine, I haven't heard from them at all.'

'Nothing in the letter?'

'Just family news, kind enquiry and Christmas greetings.'

'And, forgive me, no brushes with the police since they pulled you out of the river?'

'Not a thing.'

'And, forgive me again – no, er, private conduct with other chaps?'

I sighed wearily and said: 'There has been nothing of that kind for over two years. Nothing. I think that might be a thing of the past. Water under the bridge.'

'All right. I'm sorry, I had to ask. You see – and Violet doesn't know this because she was out shopping when it happened, so please don't say anything – but a chap came to visit me this morning at the barracks. He asked a few innocuous questions about my work there and then, this afternoon, he came and spoke to me here, in this room.'

'Who was he? Was he asking about me?'

'No, he just asked a few questions about me and Violet, nothing impertinent – how long we'd lived here, that sort of thing.'

'Was he some sort of insurance salesman?'

'No, he wasn't – and he was quite genuine. He showed me his papers. He was a detective from Scotland Yard.'

7

'Ladies and gentlemen, it gives me great pleasure and pride to introduce to you The Sons of Toil. This is a new charity set up with an endowment from my company to assist the Unemployed Man. Many of you will know of and will have written about The Maidens of Mercy, of which Lady Outhwaite is President. That splendid charitable organisation has assisted and rescued women of all ages suffering from hardship …'

So far Sir Reginald Outhwaite had not said anything that was new to anyone in the room and so the assembled journalists took another sip of coffee or dessert wine and secreted yet more *petits fours* into their pockets "for later". Some of those present had been unprepared for the magnificence of the recently opened Savoy Hotel and looked slightly dowdy amidst the glittering splendour of the private dining-room. I know I did, but did not feel too self-conscious as Adriana and I, representing an Outhwaite interest, had been tactfully put on a less prominent table at the far end from the speaker's dais.

This was the first time I had seen Sir Reginald, but the great industrialist was not an easy man to see standing, as he did, at five foot four inches tall. As his wife was five foot ten and a half, the couple were never photographed together and rarely appeared together in public. On this occasion her ladyship sat regally throughout the proceedings hosting a table of London correspondents, while her husband's table catered for journalists from northern industrial cities. I had been placed next to the editor of *The Stage*, the journal for the perennially unemployed.

'But why should the stronger sex be overlooked, ladies and gentlemen?' Sir Reginald continued, looking up from his notes on the lectern and allowing his Lancastrian tones to clear the acoustic of the room. This allowed for a dramatic pause and he looked like an indignant frog in a tactfully tailored morning suit. His bulbous grey eyes took in the audience and his grey hair quivered self-righteously. 'The fact is that no matter how many charities this country has, or how many philanthropists there are – and there aren't that many, let me tell you – the advances in science and technology which have helped make this country great are proceeding too rapidly for the ordinary working man to keep up – and there's only so much money to spare for new scholarships and apprenticeships. And all the while, those who have been fortunate enough to stay abreast of the times and who have profited, flaunt their wealth regardless of how such display inflames social unrest and promotes envy and distrust between the social orders.'

I noticed Adriana smiling wryly as she discreetly observed the design and provenance of the silverware. She had already taken copious notes about the curtain fabric and wallpaper. Even as Sir Reginald spoke, the sceptical glances of other journalists were taking in the superb chandeliers lit by the new electricity. Others stared down at the floor, slightly embarrassed, and became entranced by the patterns of the lustrous Persian carpets at their feet. I saw the words "He's after a peerage" distinctly mouthed at a colleague by an earnest-looking gentleman in a corduroy suit. None of this would affect what I was going to write and I was waiting for what came next.

'I want to help The Sons of Toil – provided they will help themselves. And they need to be taught how to do that. So I will be inviting two hundred men each month to Outhwaite Towers for the day. Their return train fare will be provided; they will receive an attendance allowance of sixpence and be given two meals. And they will be inspired and given hope by a series of lectures in the morning and afternoon on the following subjects: "The Influence of a Permanent Income on Thought"; "Keeping the Nose to the Grindstone"...'

By this time quite a few pencils were scribbling, including my own. The more experienced correspondents, however, simply looked at the printed information leaflet that had been handed to each guest on arrival, to check that they need not bestir themselves. I had just caught up with Sir Reginald's leading points when I noticed that Adriana was no longer at the table. Of course, her remit was not confined to the dining-room or The Sons of Toil so I imagined she was taking in other splendours of the Savoy.

'Begging your pardon, sir,' a hotel page was standing beside me proffering a folded piece of paper on a salver, 'I was asked to give you this.'

Taking the note, I read: "Am inspecting Suite 601 on the sixth floor with the management's permission. Please join me, but be discreet. A.C."

*

35

Waiting for the ascending chamber beside me was a tall, broad gentleman in an astrakhan coat. His hair was long and wavy and in his right hand he carried a cane adorned with an elegant pommel. It was the writer Oscar Wilde. I would have recognised him anywhere from his photograph. There was an inscribed one of these on the wall in Lady Outhwaite's office.

'You do not look like a Son of Toil to me, sir,' he said in his faintly scented, Dublin-dulcet drawl. 'Do I perceive a fellow gentleman of letters?'

'Yes, Mr Wilde, you do,' I replied, 'though not as celebrated as you are.'

'"Time, time, time," to quote the Bard. One of his more laconic lines, is it not? After you, please.' He gestured that I should enter the ascending chamber ahead of him. Apart from the attendant, who asked us which floors we required, Mr Wilde and I were the only passengers.

'We are all Sons of Toil, Mr …?'

'Maitheson,' I supplied.

'Well, Mr Maitheson, we are all Sons of Toil as we strive towards the Parnassus of perfection.'

'I have only just begun to climb the mountain, Mr Wilde.'

'Do not be afraid to fall, sir. The basis of optimism is sheer terror. Ah! We have reached the fourth floor.' The doors were opened and he stepped out. 'You see,' he smiled at me, 'already you are about to climb higher than me. Good day to you.'

*

Adriana was sitting at the window, looking out over the Thames and sipping champagne. The sky was still, sharp and without a cloud. Early afternoon sun blazed straight into my eyes as I gazed out over the sparkling river. I had never before seen the centre of London from such a height. Myriad wisps of smoke hung daintily over hundreds of different chimneys. There was no fog and no foliage to blur the details of the great buildings that rose up proudly to right and left: St Paul's Cathedral to the east with Southwark Cathedral further downriver; over in the west the be-pinnacled Palace of Westminster, the neo-Venetian facades of St. Thomas's Hospital and, still further upstream, Lambeth Palace looking like castellated fudge.

This was fairyland seen from a cocoon of luxury, the like of which I had never experienced: all-embracing deep warmth, sumptuous fabrics, fresh flowers and soothing quiet in the country's grandest hotel. It was a very different feeling to the luxury of the few grand houses I had been in. Here the atmosphere was liberating and permissive. It was as though anything was allowed to happen because it was nobody's home. Anything might happen.

Adriana looked up at me. 'The manager was too obliging when I told him of my journalistic mission,' she said. 'He insisted on the bottle of champagne. There's only one glass. Will you share it with me?' She held it up.

I couldn't resist accepting the glass and taking a sip. 'You will get me into trouble,' I said, taking another, larger sip.

'No, I won't. You know how it stands between Margarita and Papa. I'll protect you.'

'Miss Creston, what do you want of me?'

She stood up, took the glass from me, put it on the side table and came very close.

'You do know, don't you?' I whispered.

'I know, or at any rate I have had my suspicions, and I don't care. It is only the middle classes who worry about such matters.'

'I'm "middle class" and I do worry, I admit.'

'But Richard, is it something about which you are truly happy?'

'No. How can I be? It's against the law for one thing.'

'If it were not against the law, is it what you really want?'

'I don't know. I've never … had the opportunity … I've … never met a girl with whom I might want to go to bed.'

'And I've never met a man, or woman, with whom I might want to go to bed. Until now.'

I closed my eyes. I felt Adriana take my hand and kiss it. Acceptance – here was acceptance; of my girlish looks by a girl; of my musical and sensitive temperament that aroused jealousy from the untalented and vulgar; of my diffident good manners that invited the selfish and the boorish to take advantage; of my modest income that gave some wealthier people the notion that their contumely was not noticed and remembered.

Adriana put my hand around her waist and we kissed – and this led to all the arousal, fumblings, laughter and ecstasies of the time-honoured rite of passage.

We were so high above London that we did not find it necessary to close the curtains.

8

December 9th, 1890

Dear Miss Maitheson,
One of our coachmen is in the habit of putting a small pot of wild flowers
in the tack room at our stables in Norfolk. We think that he may be a
Decadent. How are we to find out and what action do you advise if our
suspicions prove to be correct?
  I remain yours,
  The Dowager Countess of Beeston.

December 12th, 1890

Dear Lady Beeston,
Your question is a delicate one. Does the coachman frighten the horses?
Much may be discovered by that. If he does, then he is obviously not suited
to a situation in the stables.
  Yours sincerely,
  Miss Maitheson.

December 9th, 1890

Dear Miss Maitheson,
We intend to hold a reception in—

'Yes, Mrs Jones, what is it?' I asked wearily. I had been at the office
very early that morning so as to type my report on the previous day.

Mrs Jones said nothing, but looked at me keenly.

'Well?'

Still the old woman said nothing. Then she narrowed her eyes and gave a
knowing smile. I wanted to club her to death with the typewriter. She was
the epitome of prurient provincialism. I couldn't understand why Lady
Outhwaite employed her. I supposed it was because Mrs Jones' wages
were minimal. Now she cringed and simpered before delivering her
message: 'In the Boardroom, if you please, Mr Maitheson.'

Thankfully the report on The Sons of Toil had been submitted in good time and I was on top of the "Letters" page. I had nothing to fear, or so I thought. Mrs Jones suddenly gave a little giggle and said: 'The Tribunal of Transgression is waiting.'

'"The Tribunal of Transgression"?'

'You've not attended one of those before, have you? Haven't been here long enough. Well, there's always a *first* time.'

With a heavy heart I gathered up my notepad and pencil and ascended the stairs. An eerie silence pervaded all the offices. The typewriters were still. The chattering had ceased. Soon I realised that this was so as much of the meeting as possible might be overheard. When I arrived at the Boardroom the first words I heard were from Lady Outhwaite: ' You may leave the door open, Mr Maitheson, and Mr Wilkins, please direct the speaking trumpet into the middle of the room.'

I sat down at the end of the long table. Stony-faced dowagers, matrons and earnest debutantes were ranged along either side as usual. The editor sat at his console table looking nervously at his shoes. At the far end of the expanse of mahogany Lady Outhwaite sat enthroned in a gown of deepest green, a cluster of emeralds sparkling malevolently from a giant brooch. Her lorgnette was trained downwards at a portfolio of papers. Adriana sat next to her quite composed, her expression betraying nothing. I wanted to gaze and gaze at her, to dive and slide along the table to hold her hands and embrace her. As it was, I avoided her eye and decided that the situation was best conducted with the tiniest sliver of ice in my heart.

Lady Outhwaite began in a slow, very clear voice: 'As you will be aware, ladies and gentlemen, today is Tuesday the 12th of December and the Carol Concert takes place a week today.' With the delicious deliberation of the powerful she opened her portfolio and looked at the first piece of paper in the pile. 'You will recall that at last Tuesday's meeting I asked you to endeavour to sell a hundred tickets between you and I have here a tally of your efforts to date. Shall we begin with the most commendable results? And shall we then work our way down to the purlieus of perfidy and indolence? I think we shall.'

Mrs Jones, who was now standing beside Lady Outhwaite's chair smiled grimly. Most of the other listeners by now had allowed their spirits to plunge into, and then wallow in, the shallows of dread as her ladyship began: 'Caroline, (The Lady Caroline Hillbury, "Reports on Weddings") congratulations, you have sold twelve tickets. Well done. And Mr Wilkins, you have also acquitted yourself honourably in mustering a dozen takers from the press rooms. Let us now consider the lesser achievements. Victoria,' (Mrs Lawrence Williamson, "Social News") 'and Sarah,' (Mrs Gregory Flint-Gowry, "Educating Our Girls") 'eight tickets each. Elizabeth,' (Lady Lambe-Weston, "The Musical Year") 'six tickets and the Misses Anderson' ("Recommended"), 'Norris' ("International News") 'and Benedict' ("Our Young People's Page"): 'four tickets *between them.*'

There Lady Outhwaite paused and stared around the table. The ominous silence allowed a cloud of guilt to develop and be given time to settle upon the remaining dozen people in the room whose names had not been read out. I did not consider it a good idea to remark that I was "volunteering" my services for the concert and that I did not move in the circles wealthy enough to afford the price of the tickets. I kept my nerve and stayed silent. One or two ladies nervously ventured that it was a busy time of year, but that they would still keep trying. Then the true horror of the meeting began.

The Gentlewoman's Poetess, Augusta Hantry, was a thin, nervous widow in her fifties. She wore spectacles with large lenses and affected gowns of the "Aesthetic" style, billowing creations printed with flowers and foliage. These were overlaid by a plethora of knitted scarves in cold weather. She was highly strung and not accustomed to pressure of any kind.

'I can't bear it, Margarita,' she wailed. 'I can't bear this oppressive atmosphere.'

'To what do you allude, Augusta?' Lady Outhwaite replied icily.

'How do you expect me to sell tickets *and* write a Christmas poem?' the Poetess complained in anguished tones.

'I'm glad you brought up the subject of the Christmas poem, Augusta. I think I have your second attempt at an offering here.' Her ladyship brought out a manuscript from the portfolio. 'Shall we consider it together? Shall we? I think we shall.'

Nobody could bear to look at Mrs Hantry as Lady Outhwaite cleared her throat, took a deep breath of pleasure and—

'No, Margarita, please,' Adriana intervened, snatching the paper and running down the room to the unhappy Poetess. 'I don't think there's any need to humiliate Mrs Hantry further. If you don't like the poem then it's your right to ask Mr Wilkins to remove it, but we none of us wish for this persecution.'

I don't think anyone else was in a position to have stood up to Lady Outhwaite in that way. Only someone who had nothing to lose could have done it.

Now the unfortunate Augusta started sobbing. 'Mrs Hantry,' said Adriana gently, 'please don't upset yourself. Perhaps you would care to wait downstairs with me. My father's carriage will be here soon. I could take you home, or else you might like to have lunch at Cormanston House with me and Mama. She has always liked your verses.'

'Thank you, dear,' sniffed the Poetess. 'You are very kind. I think I should like that very much.' Mustering her dignity she rose to her feet and addressed Lady Outhwaite: 'You are a common bully, madam – you and your pompous gnome of a husband. You shall not see me here again. And if you are singing at the Carol Concert it shall end in catastrophe.'

'Jones,' Lady Outhwaite snapped, 'go to the office library at once. There you shall find a copy of Mrs Hantry's mercifully very slim volume of verse. Remove it immediately to the Dark Cupboard.'

'To the Dark Cupboard, your ladyship?' Mrs Jones whispered ecstatically.

'To the Dark Cupboard.' The servant bustled out with malicious self-importance. 'And you, Miss Creston, might care to come to my office tomorrow morning after the Inspection.'

Adriana nodded and led Augusta out in silence.

There was a collective exhaling of breath in the Boardroom and Lady Outhwaite continued to give orders smoothly: 'Kindly remove the poem, Mr Wilkins. We will use the space for an advertisement for the Concert. I will supply the text this afternoon.'

'Very good, my lady.'

'This does not mean,' her ladyship warned, 'that you who have not been named may relax your efforts to sell tickets. And so we come to the Tribunal of Transgression. Mr Maitheson, you stand accused so please stand.'

I could feel myself blushing as I rose to my feet. 'Lady Outhwaite?'

'Mr Maitheson, you are very much on probation, as you know.'

'Yes, my lady.'

'It is fortunate that your work continues to give satisfaction. The report on The Sons of Toil luncheon is excellent and I was pleased by your letter to the little boy about the dinosaurs.'

'Thank you, my lady.'

'However, yesterday, at the Savoy, you were *seen*.'

'Yes, my lady. I was not aware of any blind persons being present.'

'I do not tolerate impertinence of any kind, Mr Maitheson. The fabric of Society is deference. Its structure is maintained by the rivets of respect.'

'Yes, my lady.'

'As I say, you were seen. Perhaps you would care to confess your transgression.'

I really could not imagine to what Lady Outhwaite was referring. Had she, after lunch, risen up over London in a hot air balloon with a telescope? Had she scaled the balconies of the Savoy, like an enormous be-jewelled ape, and peered in at the windows of Suite 601?

At this point Mrs Jones, anxious not to miss anything, returned breathlessly. She heard me say: 'My lady, I am at a loss to know what my transgression is or was. Perhaps you would be kind enough to explain.'

'Mr Maitheson, it pains me to be explicit. That is for the unimaginative, but on this occasion I shall consort with Truth. You were seen with Mr Oscar Wilde.'

'Yes, my lady,' I ventured slowly. 'I did speak to that gentleman.'

'And you went upstairs with him in the ascending chamber?'

'Yes, Lady Outhwaite, I did.'

Now the listeners sat with their mouths a little open, transfixed by the prospect of a scandal served up for their especial delight. I could feel the pressure of invisible ears pressed to doors and walls around the building. I sensed the jockeying for proximity to the speaking trumpet down in the basement.

'Would you care to continue?' Lady Outhwaite purred.

Suddenly I realised why these ladies, why Society tolerated this dreadful woman. She was a great entertainer in the "bread and circuses" tradition of ancient Rome. Her instinct for identifying a victim was certain. Her understanding of human appetites was complete.

'Well, my lady ...'

'Yes?'

'Well, as you know, Mr Wilde resigned the editorship of *The Woman's World* last year and the magazine closed down. So when I saw him in the lobby of the Savoy, I felt that here was my chance to secure an interview with him, for this journal, on the subject of his experiences editing a magazine for ladies. Our readers would surely appreciate such a piece, wouldn't they?'

Yes, they would, I thought. But would they be allowed it?

Lady Outhwaite's owlish eyes looked into mine unflinchingly. 'Mr Maitheson,' she said, 'you are young and untutored in the ways of Society, not being part of it yourself. But I commend your flair for journalism. You show great promise in the field and I believe you will succeed in it. However, in acquitting you of all charges and assuring you of your situation here, I give you this warning. Mr Oscar Wilde is an extremely dangerous man. He is a subversive commentator who undermines the sacred edifice which supports Her Majesty the Queen-Empress. He is a corruptor of youth and, in particular, of good-looking young men such as you. His social stock, as Sir Reginald would express it, is "close to top of the market". You are advised now, by me, from whom no secrets are hid, never to speak to Oscar Wilde, to be in touch with him or to read his writings. Do I make myself clear?'

'Yes, Lady Outhwaite, you do.'

'Very well. Ladies and gentlemen, the meeting is at an end. Jones, you are drooping like a disappointed vulture. I know, you have scented blood and been cheated of it. So be consoled: you know the photograph of Oscar Wilde in my office?'

'Yes, my lady?' the creature twittered hopefully. 'The Dark Cupboard?'

'Yes, Jones. Childe Oscar to the Dark Cupboard comes.'

9

St. Paul's Church was packed on the night of the Carol Concert. The extra advertisement in *The Gentlewoman* had encouraged sales, as had Lady Outhwaite's cajoling in the Boardroom. Even I had managed to sell two tickets, to Arthur and Violet. Above all the weather was dry and clear. A foul night would have deterred a Society audience even if they had already parted with their money. By half-past seven Bedford Street and Henrietta Street were lined with carriages as the affluent do-gooders made their way along the flambeau-lit path through the cemetery and up the semi-circle of steps into the church.

In the vestibule they were greeted effusively by Father Grantley and Lady Outhwaite, who seemed to know "everybody". Mr Wilkins and Adriana presided over a reception table to ensure that there were no mix-ups with the tickets. Once through the glass-panelled double doors, the spectacle was of seasonal cheer on the grand scale: banks of candles, gleaming satellites of chandeliers; refulgent gilt frames; beeswax-polished pews; and, most comforting of all, the soft scent of pine from an enormous Christmas tree. The church was not cold, either, for the heating pipes had been working overtime all afternoon.

If I had not been nervous at the prospect of accompanying my employer in a difficult aria I would have been enjoying myself. There is more pressure on a performer if loved ones are in the audience and it had been many months since I had played in front of anyone. We had had three rehearsals in the church over the past week, so I had become used to the grand piano and Lady Outhwaite to the acoustics. She had sung the aria before, knew the words perfectly, but her technique was not that of a trained singer. Her number would be the last item in the first half of the concert immediately before the interval. It was hoped privately by all who knew of her ladyship's musical reputation that the prospect of the lavish refreshments to follow her performance would sustain the audience's good will and good manners.

From my vantage point at the piano, next to the raised area on which the orchestra sat, I could see the intense concentration on the faces of the string players as they played the thrilling runs of the introduction. The mounting tension galvanised everyone: audience; choristers along each side of the dais; the patiently waiting soloists. Two of these, the tenor and the bass Stuardo Baritoni, sat in the middle of the platform immediately in front of the band. Lady Outhwaite sat next to me on the lower level so that she could more easily move across to the end of the central aisle, thus displaying her gown more advantageously.

With superb aplomb Signor Baritoni rose for his entrance and began the dramatic homily: "Why do the nations so furiously rage together; why do the people imagine a vain thing?" His demeanour and delivery were magnificent, his whole frame shaking with the anger of an ancient prophet. If it had been the correct custom to clap between the arias of an oratorio he would certainly have been applauded. The concert had opened well and it proceeded smoothly and pleasurably all the way through to the irrefutable splendour of the Hallelujah Chorus. For this the audience followed the Hanoverian tradition of standing. At its close, as everyone resumed their seats, I began playing the sublime opening of *I know that my Redeemer liveth* and Lady Outhwaite glided serenely into position at the centre of the church, a towering presence in burgundy and gold.

She began confidently, effortlessly covering the first interval to the high "know", but very gradually she started to let the tempo drag. Father Grantley had been right when he said that the aria was interminable. Just as we reached "And tho' worms destroy this body" a sound of breaking glass came from the rear of the church. Most people assumed a goblet had fallen off one of the buffet tables; the musicians present probably thought that the Almighty was commenting on Lady Outhwaite's singing. Everyone looked round fleetingly. Those nearest the source of the noise, however, gasped in horror. Only they could see that one of the glass panels in the double doors had been broken and that the barrel of a revolver was protruding through the jagged aperture.

The explosion of the gunshot made me freeze, then duck down on my stool before scrambling to the floor. I heard gasps, screams, moans and shouts all intermingled. Lady Outhwaite had sunk slowly to the ground. The entire audience was cowering between the pews. Orchestra and chorus, music, chairs and instruments were scattered all over the platform where people lay huddled, crouching, flattened and trembling. Surveying the scene you would have thought a volley of rounds had been fired, causing carnage, not a solitary shot.

The silence of profound horror followed, but you could sense the unspoken thoughts. What was it? Who had caused it? Had anyone been hit? Would it happen again? Was it safe to move or make a sound?

'Miss Creston?' I called out, 'Mr Wilkins?' There was no response. 'Arthur? Violet?'

'It's all right, Richard, we're all right,' my brother called back.

This exchange opened the floodgates as others overcame their shock and asked after loved ones and friends. Now came the muffled sobbing of relief, more concerned enquiries and ever louder speculation and expressions of outrage.

'Is there a doctor here?' a man in the orchestra shouted. 'Signor Baritoni's been shot.'

'I'm a doctor. Stay there.' This from a man in the audience.

'And please see to my wife whilst you're about it.' This was the voice of Sir Reginald Outhwaite. 'I suggest everyone else stay still.'

'Not bloody likely, Outhwaite. Someone needs to see if he's still there. I'll do it. I've got a gun.'

I didn't know who this other man was, but he sounded as if he may have once been a soldier, or was one still.

So as not to make himself a target the medical man had started crawling towards the concert platform from half-way down the northern side aisle. I could hear him getting closer. Meanwhile, from the opposite side aisle came the sounds of scuttling as the gentleman with a firearm made his way towards the double doors through which the audience had entered.

'Keep down, doctor, until I've checked outside,' he shouted. Suddenly he was heard running up to the wall alongside the doors and then heard recovering his breath. His gasps were audible all down the church. Then, after an agonising silence, I heard him hurl himself at the doors. There was a tinkling of glass as loose shards fell to the floor, followed by a low scraping as if a heavy wooden object was being pushed across the tiles. Everyone held their breath, dreading further shots or some cry. We heard footsteps and then a shout of 'It's all right. He's gone. All clear.'

Now the unknown physician got up and ran to Baritoni, who had tipped backwards in his chair into the musician who had called for help. The singer was still in his chair, facing upwards but quite motionless. A bullet hole blackened his forehead, from which dark blood trickled. The doctor had taken off his own coat and was covering the dead man's face and chest with it.

'Ladies and gentlemen, I'm sorry,' he announced. 'There's nothing to be done. Could you all please stand away and could one of you go for an ambulance?'

This the musician who had caught Baritoni undertook to do. I turned and ran past Lady Outhwaite, who was now being revived with *sal volatile*, and up the central aisle to the double doors at the end. I had to push through quite a crowd to reach the vestibule where I was just in time to see Father Grantley guiding four gentlemen into the vestry. They were carrying the bodies of Mr Wilkins and Adriana.

10

ST. PAUL'S CHURCH OUTRAGE

London Society is outraged by the killing on Tuesday evening, 19th December, of Signor Stuardo Baritoni during a carol concert at St. Paul's Church, Covent Garden.

Signor Baritoni, the former House Manager of the Royal Italian Opera House, had just sung an aria from The Messiah when he was shot with a single bullet from a revolver whilst sitting on the concert platform. A doctor in the audience, who declined to be named, was able to attend to the wounded man shortly after the shooting and pronounced him as dead immediately. An ambulance was called for and soon the body of Signor Baritoni was taken away to be examined by investigating surgeons at Scotland Yard.

A number of witnesses reported seeing the barrel of a revolver protruding through a broken glass panel in a door at the rear of the church leading to the vestibule. The glass panel had been smashed by the assassin in order to take the shot but was too small to allow any view of the assailant's face or body. The door was subsequently found to have been barricaded by a table in the vestibule in order to hamper pursuit.

Only two people inside the church could have seen the killer. They were the Hon. Adriana Creston, only daughter of Viscount Cormanston, and Mr Thomas Wilkins, editor of The Gentlewoman. These two persons had been on duty in the vestibule after the concert began to attend to latecomers and to keep watch over the takings. It was whilst Mr Wilkins had been locking these away in the vestry that Miss Creston was approached from behind and smothered with a pad of chloroform. She never saw her attacker and was unconscious by the time Mr Wilkins returned to the vestibule and was himself disabled from behind in the same manner. Both Miss Creston and Mr Wilkins recovered consciousness an hour later.

The vicar of St. Paul's, the Reverend Giles Grantley, was amongst the audience when the shooting took place. He has confirmed that, apart from the glass panel, the church was not damaged in any way and that nothing was stolen.

The concert was being held to benefit The Maidens of Mercy, the charity of which Lady Outhwaite, wife of the industrialist Sir Reginald Outhwaite, is President. Her ladyship is reported to be devastated by the catastrophe, though pleased that so much money was raised by the generosity of the large audience. The concert was immediately abandoned.

The Gentlewoman and The Maidens of Mercy beg leave to offer their deepest condolences and sympathy to the family and friends of Signor Baritoni. An obituary of that gentleman will appear in the New Year.

RICHARD MAITHESON

Lady Outhwaite was dressed completely in black and stood in solitary solemnity as Mr Wilkins, Father Grantley and I were ushered into the Boardroom. We three were also in mourning attire and were the only ones admitted to the Inspection that Wednesday before Christmas. Confidentiality and discretion were vital, so Mrs Jones was not allowed to be present. Adriana had been ordered to stay at home by her parents, who were concerned for her safety and anxious that she should not be pestered by the Press. The entire staff of *The Gentlewoman* had been sworn to silence, as had all the members of the charity and the company of the Opera House. It was hoped that those who had been in in the audience were not the kind of people who talked to reporters. As for the police, when eventually they attended the scene of the shooting, there was little that they could tell anyone – even if they had been allowed to make a statement – that was not summed up in my article.

Silence fell on the room as first Father Grantley, then Mr Wilkins, read my typescript. The only other person to have read it was Lady Outhwaite, who now spoke very quietly.

'Gentlemen, I trust that you find Mr Maitheson's account accurate, fair and respectful?'

'Yes, Margarita, and thank you for allowing me to read it before publication. Mr Wilkins, are you in agreement?'

'I am, Father Grantley.'

'I have been in two minds,' Lady Outhwaite mused, 'as to whether we should publish anything at all. However, I've heard from Augustus Harris that Signor Baritoni's family were informed earlier this morning – and Scotland Yard can hardly object. There are hundreds of people who could tell almost exactly the same story, so it cannot interfere with their investigations. But if we are lucky *The Gentlewoman* will carry in print the best, if not the first, version of events.'

We all nodded dutifully knowing that, if she could help it, nothing would stop Lady Outhwaite from coming first in the race to break the terrible news. Given the circumstances she would be blamed if she didn't try. Now she addressed her editor: 'Mr Wilkins, would you be prepared to set up this story yourself on your own?'

'Yes, my lady.'

'Front page, centre and with a black border. You may make any adjustments elsewhere at your discretion. We have no Christmas Poem, of course.'

'Yes, my lady.'

'Very well, Mr Wilkins, you may proceed.'

*

Because of the veil of secrecy imposed on the office that day, to stay in place until publication on the Thursday morning, the staff of *The Gentlewoman* had brought in sandwiches and picnics *en masse*. That way no one had to leave the building at lunchtime. And so it came to pass that a mystery was explained to me. This was the question of what Mrs Jones did during the midday break and where she went.

I had just eaten cheese and chutney sandwiches at my desk and was about to resume work on readers' correspondence when Lady Outhwaite's drudge knocked. I bade her enter, she came in, closed the door and sat down opposite. My heart sank. On her face was an expression of supreme satisfaction.

'So ...' she said and let the word hang in what she imagined was a limbo of agonising suspense. I knew better than to show any interest in this gnomic utterance and was resigned to what I knew was coming next.

'So ...' she said again and smiled complacently. There was nothing to do but open a letter and hope that Mrs Jones' desire to impart some nugatory nugget would expand her vocabulary at some point before teatime. I began to read yet another complaint about the dinosaurs in Crystal Palace Park and had decided that there were more serious threats to Londoners' welfare when my visitor gave vent to another 'So ...'.

I should mention that because of the influence of Middlesbrough on her accent the word sounded to me like "saw".

'What did you see, Mrs Jones?' I asked.

'Not saw. *Heard* ... So ...'.

'Mrs Jones, please don't think me rude, but these monosyllabic semantics are of very limited interest. If you are hoping for news or comment relating to last night, I am not at liberty to say anything. And I am not alone. Was there something else?'

Now she was goaded into unburdening her secret: 'I was in the Dark Cupboard.'

'And where is that exactly?'

'In her ladyship's office. A big cupboard it is with a hidden door in the wall, like a linen room. I go there at lunchtimes and I go there at other times, too. I like to contemplate the sins of the world, to think about the mighty that are fallen. It's where I find Peace.'

'And you eat your lunch there in the dark?'

'Yes.'

'And Lady Outhwaite knows this?'

'Oh yes. She prefers me to be seen as little as possible.'

'And you overhear things, too, I expect.'

'Only when her ladyship forgets I'm there.'

'And what have you heard? You obviously want to tell me.'

'Well ... I suppose you know about the opera gala in February in the presence of The Prince of Wales?' she asked with an affected air of nonchalance.

'Yes.'

'*How* do you know?' Mrs Jones cried out in disappointment.

'I was there when poor Signor Baritoni told Father Grantley.'

'Oh. Well, when I was in the cupboard this morning my lady and the vicar were talking about it and she was saying she was afraid it would not now go ahead because of what happened in the church last night, and Father Grantley urged her not to cancel it but to write to His Royal Highness and suggest that the gala be in aid of The Maidens *and* of a fund for Mr Baritoni's family. The vicar felt sure this was the right thing to do because the Italian gentleman was so popular at the Opera House.'

'And Lady Outhwaite agreed?'

'She wrote the letter at once. So. You didn't know that, did you?'

I allowed Mrs Jones her claim to superior knowledge.

'And there's something else you don't know, Mr Maitheson.'

'What's that?'

'She's going to ask you to write Mr Baritoni's obituary.'

I supposed that this was because I was the only reporter at *The Gentlewoman* with whom he had any acquaintance, but I would have to find out a great deal more about him.

'And ...' Mrs Jones paused to ensure that she had my complete attention, 'there's another thing.'

'Yes?' I enquired tersely.

'Her ladyship is frightened. She's convinced that whoever shot Mr Baritoni was actually aiming at her.'

11

As well she might be, I thought as I left the office that evening. Lady Outhwaite's subdued manner at the Inspection was quite unlike her, but then she had suffered a severe blow to her prestige. She could not possibly imagine that someone had resorted to shooting her to stop her singing – could she? It was more likely that she was afraid of someone whose pride she had badly injured or whose social position she had superseded. The country must be full of such people, I reckoned. It was true that she had been standing immediately in front of the seated Mr Baritoni in the church, and on a lower level, so that their upper bodies would have been roughly at the same height from the ground. Her ladyship, however, had fainted and so had not seen the bullet wound that I had glimpsed in the centre of Baritoni's forehead. It looked like the work of an expert marksman who had chosen to shoot him and not her. But why would anyone want to kill the Italian who, by all accounts, had been one of the most popular men in London?

Under my arm, wrapped in brown paper, was a hot-off-the-press copy of the new edition of *The Gentlewoman*. I had been granted permission to deliver it in person to Cormanston House. In my pocket, wrapped in gold paper with a red ribbon bow, was a small parcel, a Christmas present for Adriana. She had told me the previous evening, as she left the church, that she would be at home.

Her family's London mansion was one of the oldest of the noble town houses. It was in Lincoln's Inn Fields, a brisk fifteen minutes' walk away. This ancient rectangle of elegance was the very first of the capital's "squares", laid out in the 17th century by Inigo Jones, who had not only designed St. Paul's, Covent Garden, but Cormanston House also. Here was a bastion of symmetry, of orange brickwork and Portland stone with balustrades and finials decorating the skyline, that flaunted the fashionable taste of an era long gone; of certainties shaken to the core by revolutions Glorious, French, American and Industrial – but whose foundations, facades and structures were resolutely secure. To all the world Cormanston

House proclaimed that its owners would stop at nothing to ensure that time stood still, for ever and in the right place.

'Commendably concise and unsensational,' Lady Cormanston remarked when she had read my report on the shooting. 'Do you not agree, Adriana?'

Mother and daughter sat on a sofa beside the magnificent marble fireplace which housed a crackling fire of logs and pinecones. Its light flickered all over the baubles on the Christmas tree that stood opposite, between two of the first floor windows that commanded the square. Mother and daughter looked exactly alike, blonde beauties both, with only an age gap of twenty-five years between them.

'I do, Mama,' Adriana replied, 'and I hope it will set the tone for the reports that follow in other journals.'

'This edition was not graced by something of your own, Miss Creston,' I ventured from my chair on the other side of the fireplace.

'Lady Outhwaite offered me the chance of writing a seasonal poem,' said Adriana, glancing at her mother, 'but I felt it would be unkind and appear too self-serving to take over the position of Poetess immediately after Mrs Hantry's dismissal.'

'Besides,' said the mother gently, 'Lord Cormanston and I have decided that *The Gentlewoman* is probably not the most suitable claimant on Miss Creston's time. You will understand, Mr Maitheson, that as a family we have to be extremely sensitive as to how we are perceived in public life. Last night's outrage at St. Paul's, notwithstanding your excellent article, will perhaps identify my daughter as someone who is a form of target.'

'For whom, Lady Cormanston?' I asked.

The viscountess looked straight into my eyes very kindly before saying carefully: 'Mr Maitheson, please forgive me for not being more explicit. I should like to confide in you very much, for you strike me as someone who respects the importance of secrets. So I know you will respect my discretion. The Empire and Society depend on certain secrets remaining safeguarded. The Outhwaites of this world may think of themselves as belonging to the ruling class, but I think you know better.'

Lady Cormanston was right. I did, but I was saddened by what I felt had been a warning and an announcement. I was not going to be seeing Adriana for some time. The suspicion was confirmed when I was informed that the family would be travelling to Ireland on the morrow to spend Christmas at Cormanston Castle in County Meath.

I was wondering how on earth I was going to give Adriana the present that I had bought. It was yet another secret to be guarded at all costs, one that might never be disclosed.

Suddenly the peace of Lincoln's Inn Fields was broken by two sharp bangs. To me they sounded like festive firecrackers, but Lady Cormanston jumped up in alarm. Instinctively she moved towards the closed curtains as if to look out, then remembered herself and turned back to the fireplace to ring the bell. I had stood up at the same time as my hostess so that I was by the Christmas tree when her back was turned. Within seconds the little gold parcel was out of my pocket and nestling amongst the decorations festooning the pine branches, hiding in plain sight. Only Adriana saw me put it there.

After the summoned servant had returned and reported that the disturbance had been attributed to some passing students, I politely offered my compliments of the season and left the mansion.

*

'God rest you merry, Gentlemen,
Let nothing you dismay;
For Jesus Christ our Saviour
Was born upon this Day
To save poor souls from Satan's power
When they had gone astray—'

'Aah, shut yer face!' A drunken yell and the slam of a door drowned out and then cut off the chorus of the carol. It was being sung along one of the courts off Vere Street, which I crossed in order to make my way along Kemble Street. This was the quickest way home but not the most pleasant, especially having just left the luxurious grandeur of Cormanston House. All around me were rundown dwellings and dirty shops. On my right were some of the worst slums of London, never to be entered except *in extremis*. The narrow alleys and close-packed houses had been notorious for decades: evil smelling, disease ridden snares of vicious criminal living. In this cold season the air was thick with smoke and continuous coughing. The importunate whispers of prostitutes or beggars assailed me from every other doorway. It was a street to be walked along as fast as possible and that is why I nearly knocked over Father Grantley as he turned into Drury Lane from Russell Street. He too was hurrying, to get out of the cold and also because he was laden down with two crates of wine and a couple of large hampers. He was clearly anxious to set them down as soon as possible.

'Oh, Mr Maitheson, thank goodness it's you,' he gasped. 'You have to be so careful in this neighbourhood. My cloth does not necessarily protect me. You couldn't possibly help me with these things, could you? There isn't far to go. I'm quite exhausted.'

The vicar was on his way to St. Agnes' Mission for destitute women a few hundred yards up Drury Lane. I readily agreed to help carry the provisions which, it transpired, were some of the untouched refreshments from the abandoned concert of the previous evening. 'Lady Outhwaite's been so generous,' he panted as we continued walking. 'She very kindly gave me leave to spread a little Christmas cheer amongst the less fortunate of the parish. I took some wine and pies to a hostel in Seven Dials this afternoon, then another load to the tenements in Parker Street. This is the last of it. The food won't keep, you see. Some of the poor people wept when they saw it, said they'd never seen food like it in their lives. Have you been over to Cormanston House?'

I told him of my delivery of the magazine and of my meeting Adriana's mother.

'A gracious lady indeed,' said Mr Grantley, 'but not one to be crossed. Oh no.'

'I don't think I've crossed her,' I said, worried that she had discovered her daughter's liaison with me. 'Why? Have you?'

'Not me personally, no, Mr Maitheson. But I know of some families who lived on their estate in Ireland. They crossed her some years ago and were evicted from their farms, had to emigrate. They ended up in Seven Dials, in fact. Sad story.'

Privately I hoped that Adriana had had no part to play in this drama of dispossession. I thought I was starting to understand why Lady Cormanston talked of her as a potential target.

We had now arrived at an old burial ground that had been converted into a public garden. Behind it stood the Church of Scotland and at either side of the garden's gates onto Drury Lane stood two redbrick buildings. The one on the right looked like a tiny chapel and was the old mortuary. The one on the left was the old lodge. It was here that the Head Keeper of St. Agnes' Mission lived. In addition to acting as a kind of porter for that grim institution he was the gatekeeper for the gardens. His little parlour was a haven of warmth and we gratefully accepted a glass of wine after we'd put the provisions down on his table.

Mr Duncan, the keeper, gave us a grin that was missing quite a few teeth and ran a gnarled hand over his unshaven chin. His thinning hair allowed a glimpse of a scalp that was lunar in its scabrousness. 'You're a proper Santa Claus, you are, Reverend,' he gurgled through a combination of wine and phlegm.

'Please don't mention it, Mr Duncan.'

'Have they caught that murderer, then? Shocking, I call it, shooting in a church.'

Father Grantley looked at the keeper sharply, then glanced at me nervously before deciding to brave it out: 'What are you talking about, man?'

'Come on, Reverend, the whole world's talking about it. At the concert last night, in your church, a man was shot dead. I've heard neighbours gossiping, shopkeepers gabbing and then ...'. Mr Duncan's face became a grotesque mask of sly cunning. He had clearly studied at the Mrs Jones Academy of Dramatic Suspense, for he paused and looked at us both searchingly and glanced around the parlour as if he imagined an audience of listeners crowded round. 'And then ... there's the *Beast*.'

The vicar looked truly alarmed and embarrassed. He could only whisper: 'What about her?'

'This shaver needs an explanation, I think,' said Mr Duncan, nodding at me. I was intrigued, I could not deny it.

'Mr Maitheson,' the vicar began, 'do you remember that on the day we first met there was a tramp lurking in the church?'

'Yes, I do. But I didn't actually see him.'

'Well, it's a "her", actually, one of the unfortunates who lodge at St. Agnes' at night, one of Mr Duncan's charges.'

'We call her "The Beast," don't we, vicar?' the keeper sniggered, 'on account of her temper and her smell and her mangy hair and her filthy nails and her breath what stinks of ...'

'Yes, all right, Mr Duncan. I am sure Mr Maitheson can imagine the poor creature. You see, Richard, the old woman has been very badly treated. She used to be a governess for a very grand family in Scotland, until about eight months ago when she was dismissed for drinking. She'd been hoping for a cottage and a pension but she got nothing. She came to London with only a passable reference and managed to find a situation in south London looking after children in a very modest household. But the fact is that she had never loved children and she liked to frighten them with tales of terror and so forth.'

Already I felt my entrails contracting. There it was again, the glimpse in my memory of the anaconda uncoiling in the muddy river.

'Father Grantley,' I asked, my mouth dry with apprehension, 'was this woman dismissed by the south London family some weeks ago, for telling stories about the dinosaurs at Crystal Palace?'

'Yes.'

'And the family in Scotland, was it the Selkirks?'

'Yes. How on earth did you know?'

'I used to work at Rockbridge Hall. I met her there.'

'Well, well, well,' Mr Duncan crowed. 'Here's a kettle of fish if you like. You're quite right, young man. That's The Beast all right – airs and graces and always going on about Hell Fire. Makes our lives a misery here, as if we ain't got enough already. Her name's Sally Jardine.'

Now that the existence of "the Beast" had been explained and acknowledged Father Grantley turned back to the gate keeper and said: 'You mentioned her in connection with the shooting, Mr Duncan.'

'Yes, vicar, I did. Because last night Sally Jardine was roaming the graveyards, like she does, and was in the one by your church just after eight o'clock. She tells me. And she also tells me that she saw the murderer going in, heard the gun shot and saw the murderer running off – everything.'

12

'And?'

'What do you mean "And?"' said Mr Duncan as he poured us all a little more wine. He was obviously relishing this chance to entertain at home, even though the good things Father Grantley and I had brought had not been intended for him.

'Mr Duncan,' the vicar persisted patiently, 'it is vital that the Be— that Sally Jardine goes to the police with her information.'

'You know her as well as I do, Reverend. Can you see her turning up at Scotland Yard? Or the detectives turning up here and getting any sense out of her?'

Father Grantley sighed in agreement. 'Then I shall have to try and reason with her. Oh dear.'

Suddenly Mr Duncan's eyes narrowed and he turned his head to one side. 'Listen,' he whispered, 'that's her!'

From outside we could hear a rasping, quavering voice intoning a dirge that I had heard before in the corridors of Rockbridge Hall: '"This ae night. This ae night, every night and all. Fire and salt and candlelight, and Christ receive thy soul."'

The same tune, the same promise of damnation filled me with dread. Would she recognise me? I thought it unlikely but would take no chances. I would stay silent and in the background.

'Could I speak to her in here, Mr Duncan?' said Father Grantley.

'Sorry, Reverend, there's strict rules against inmates in here, but I'll tell you what I'll do. I'll let you in the old mortuary. Don't worry, been empty for years. Only used to store gardening tools now. There's a couple of empty coffins you can sit on and I'll let you have a candle. Hold on, she'll need temptation.'

The keeper opened a second bottle of wine and went to the door that opened onto Drury Lane. 'Oh Sally, my love,' he called with heavy irony, holding out the drink. 'Oh Sally, my dove. I have a present for you ...'

The vicar and I heard a cry of 'Give me!' and then Mr Duncan went out into the street, bidding us follow. There she was, the "Nanny Selkirk" of

59

my memory, or "Miss Jardine" as she was also called, and how she had changed. She had lost a good deal of weight so that the filthy black linen dress of the former governess hung around her body in baggy swathes. Though barely sixty she looked older. Her grey hair was wildly overgrown and matted over her face. You couldn't see her grey eyes, that I remembered stared accusingly. As she lumbered over the cobbles she muttered incoherently about 'the creatures of the deep', but her mind was really on only one thing: drink.

'Now Sal,' Mr Duncan coaxed, 'your friend Father Grantley and a young friend of his would like to talk to you in private.'

Miss Jardine growled and lunged for the bottle of wine. 'Give me!' she cried again.

'Not 'til you've sat down in here,' the keeper wheedled as he lured his charge to the rusty gates of the garden, unlocked them and led the way to the former mortuary. 'Now you've been in here before, haven't you, Sal? When you got locked out that night, remember? So you know there are no ghosties. That's right, there you are,' Mr Duncan cooed as he unlocked the creaking door.

There was obviously a candle inside for the gardeners because we soon heard a match being struck and gradually a small, soft glow alleviated the gloom. And into the icy chamber Father Grantley and I followed. It smelt musty and damp but that was bearable. Thankfully it was still so dark that you couldn't see into the corners. There were cobwebs; we felt them brush our faces as we went in and saw two lidded coffins put facing each other. On one sat Miss Jardine, nursing her bottle like a baby. Between swigs she sang softly to herself, a ditty about 'little lambs'. I had an unpleasant feeling that if it had not been so cold in that place the odours of Miss Jardine would have overpowered our sensibilities. So the vicar and I shivered and were grateful.

'Here's the key, Reverend. Any trouble, just lock her in here and I'll fetch her later.'

I remained standing by the door so that I was hidden by Father Grantley's shadow as he sat down opposite the old woman. 'Now Sally,' he began gently, 'you are not in any trouble, you know. I just—'

'We are *ALL* in trouble,' Miss Jardine roared. 'For are we not sinners at the Brig o' Dread? Waiting for the phantoms of Beelzebub to cast us down into the *Pit*?'

'Well yes, I suppose we are in a way-'

'And shall we not writhe and scream in the never-cooling flames of *Judgement*?'

'That may be—'

'And shall not the fat folks of Babylon cry out for mercy but receive *NONE*?'

'Yes, they shall. And I know you have been wronged by them, but take comfort, Sally. They shall perish in the flames and at thine own hand.'

'Shall they, Reverend?' Miss Jardine whispered. 'Shall I find comfort?'

'Yes, my dear, you shall. And I am here to tell you how.'

The disgraced governess took a deep pull at her wine and smiled roguishly at the vicar. 'Tell me,' she whispered.

'I want you to remember last night when you were outside my church.'

'I heard music, but not clearly, for the doors of the temple were closed.'

'And did you see someone come up to the doors and go in?'

'I did. He was tall and in a black coat with a black hat and a black scarf around his face.'

'And how could you tell it was a man, Sally?' They were like children playing a game of "questions and answers". Father Grantley had obviously found a knack before this of getting on her amenable side and guiding her into lucidity.

'From the way he walked. And he coughed like a man.'

'And he went inside. Did he close the door?'

'Yes, he did, so I couldn't see anything.'

'And when did you hear the shot?'

'Five minutes or so after he went in.'

'And after that?'

'The door of the temple opened and he ran away.'

'Up the path through the churchyard?'

'No. He ran away to the right.'

'Towards Henrietta Street?'

'Yes.'

'And he had closed the door of the church behind him?'

'Yes, Father, he had.'

'Well done, Sally. Thank you. You will be saved in the eyes of the Lord and I don't think you will have to talk to the police. I'm expecting them later this evening at the Rectory and I will pass on what you have said.'

'And shall I be spared the *Pit*, Father? And the demons of Dunkeld?'

Father Grantley assured her that she would and we all three left that terrible place together.

13

No.28, Eland Road,
Battersea,
London S.W.
Boxing Day, 1890

My dear Adriana,
It feels so strange to be writing to you, partly because work has me writing to strangers all day long, but mainly because I have never written a "love letter" before. I almost feel that I should be addressing you as "Miss Creston" lest some guardian angel of Society swoop down on me for committing a solecism. Somehow, by writing you a letter, you have become more real to me, even though you are absent. I think this is because I am still in an incredulous, happy daze that we have each other and have found such happiness together – even though it was just on that one occasion at the Savoy.

How could we have been so daring and taken such a risk? Perhaps it is because we are both, in our different ways, "outside" Society, feeling that we don't quite fit in with what might be conventionally expected of us. And yet, despite the danger involved in what we did, how I wish we could do it again! Or even be able to communicate openly with one another without feeling we are continually being watched. That one time is the only time we have been alone together, completely alone. I hate the secrecy that must protect our affair more than anything: because of the strictures of working at The Gentlewoman; because of your being not yet of age and the certain fury of your family. I accept it of course – but I hate it because it reminds me of that way of life that I have left behind where secrecy was essential. And you hate it too, don't you? There is only so much pleasure to be gained from the frisson of a cloak-and-dagger liaison.

When your mother told me that you would no longer be working at the magazine and when she looked at me when I asked for whom you might be "a target", I could not help feeling that it was me that she was afraid of, or a suitor like me. You haven't told her about us, have you? She hasn't found out our secret, has she? I can only hope that I kept my countenance sufficiently so as not to give anything away, but unlike Lady Outhwaite, who claims to be omniscient, I sense that Lady Cormanston really is one "from whom no secrets are hid".

Did she, your father, or some eagle-eyed servant spot my present in the Christmas tree? And did you collect it safely? And did you like it? It was the only way I could express what I feel towards you and now I wonder if I shall ever see you again.

This thought, I have to confess, has not made my Christmas a very happy one and I hope yours has been happier. I am alone today because Arthur and Violet have gone to spend the day with my parents in Coulsdon, but yesterday we were a cheerful trio here. This was partly thanks to your wonderful present, which I found where you hid it in the office. I have always been fond of Gilbert and Sullivan's songs, as you know, and we had great fun in the parlour yesterday dipping into the beautifully bound collection and playing our favourites. It brought back some happy memories of my career as an entertainer and gave us all great pleasure. Thank you for it. The only sounds of hilarity today are from some children out in the road, which is quite iced over, sliding down the hill on tin trays.

I am sure you will want to hear all the news from Covent Garden. The fresh developments began almost immediately after I left you at Cormanston House. I ran into Father Grantley distributing left-over food and drink from the concert and we encountered a terrible drunken old woman who claimed to have seen whoever shot Mr Baritoni running away from St. Paul's. She was quite sure that it had been a tall man dressed in black. Like you she didn't see his face. Her information was relayed to the police that same evening by Mr Grantley.

The next day was extremely busy at the magazine. As Lady Outhwaite had hoped, we had stolen a march on everyone and were the first to publish the terrible news. There was a rush for copies and an extra print run was ordered. Journalists from other papers called and telegraphed all day long, but they were just referred to Scotland Yard who have not released any news at all. So speculation and rumour are running riot, with Italian secret societies strongly suspected. I have written to the Opera House requesting an interview so as to be able to write Mr Baritoni's obituary but so far have received no response. I hope the management will assist me. I haven't the time to run around ferreting out his life story.

To add to my workload, I have taken over as pianist for the services at St. Paul's Church. On the Friday of last week, just after the office had closed for Christmas, I was in The Bedford Head having a festive drink with Mr Wilkins and some of the others. In rushed Mr Grantley, who had suspected our whereabouts, and begged me to play the piano for his services on the Sunday, Christmas Eve. It transpired that his usual pianist had a severe cold and was "saving herself" for Christmas Day. (The organ has been out of order for years, apparently.) So I agreed. The music was straightforward enough and all went well. After the midnight mass was finished he asked if I might consider playing at other services because the lady with the cold was becoming unreliable; ill health and family dramas had caused such crises in the past. There is a modest stipend for the post and so I was tempted to accept the offer. Mr Grantley was so grateful that he gave me the hansom cab fare home. He asked me to start this coming Sunday. At this rate I shall become a gentleman of means and be able to ask for your hand in marriage …

Will you be tempted by the proposal? Will I see you again to be able to ask you? Will you write to me from the castle of the fairy-tale princess?

Whatever should come to pass, I want you to know how very happy you have made me. In the new decade to come I shall be a very different person, a much happier person than I was in the previous one. This is thanks to you, my darling.

With all my love, Richard.

*

Cormanston Castle,
Cormanston,
County Meath,
Ireland.
December 30th, 1890

My darling Richard,
As you can see from this letter, I was able to retrieve your beautiful present from the Christmas tree in London and without being seen. A Waterman reservoir pen! It is exquisite, such a pleasure to hold and so lovely to gaze upon with its delicately engraved "A". I love writing with it and have used it frequently already – in secret, of course, so as not to expose myself to parental comment. I would have written to you sooner, but wished to be

able to respond to any letter that came from you, as well as thanking you for a gift that will always have a hallowed place in my heart.

I am sorry that our separation spoilt your Christmas. It spoilt mine too and I entirely agree with what you say about having to keep our attachment secret, but I see no immediate solution to the problem. All through the dinners, services, parties and games here I thought only of you and although I have not spoken of you to anyone, I think that Mama does suspect there is something between you and me and, yes, I believe that was behind my removal from The Gentlewoman. *However, even if my literary ambitions are thwarted there, I have your wonderful present to keep me company and the Muse alive. "The pen is mightier than the sword." I shall simply conceal my writing materials as Jane Austen was said to do – but at least I will not die an "old maid" as she did.*

There is another matter, however, a very serious one, connected to what Mama spoke of when you came to Cormanston House. She spoke of my being a possible "target" in another sense also and you must not resent the way I write about this. Do not be jealous of the cryptic style I must adopt now. There are certain things I must both tell you about and conceal from you. Please understand that I have to express myself with great care as well as with great love.

As a family that is part of the ruling class in Ireland we are frightened. Even during the season of "peace and goodwill" rocks were thrown at our carriages as we went to church or attended social functions in the county. Do you remember how Mama jumped up in alarm when she heard those firecrackers outside the house in London? The shooting of Mr Baritoni – in a church of all places, where nobody was present but in order to raise money for impoverished women – shocked my parents deeply. We simply do not know where we are safer, here or in Town. We suspect the Post Office here of opening our mail and telegrams. And I cannot write to you at this address in Battersea again lest it put you or me in danger.

Dear Richard, how well do you know your Shakespeare? There is a line in Cymbeline *where the hero thinks of his beloved far away and who is possibly dead: "O Imogen! I'll speak to thee in silence." For the time being that is how we must communicate, but there is another line from Shakespeare which you also need to know, from* The Winter's Tale: *"It is requir'd you do awake your faith."*

That seems so bossy at first reading, doesn't it? I think it is an unnecessary injunction as far as we are concerned. I believe we have great faith in each other. I just love the line – as I love you.

With every fond wish for happiness in the year to come,
Adriana.

14

Covent Garden was an area which was dominated by, and looked up to, the Opera House. Its grandeur and international reputation had put the locality on the map of the world. Its near neighbours The Theatre Royal, Drury Lane and the Lyceum Theatre, were celebrated too but had not presented the British premières of some of the world's greatest composers – and Augustus Harris, the Opera House's impresario, had after all graduated from Drury Lane. In the eyes of the Empire, Barry's 1858 temple to music and Queen Victoria represented the apogee of civilisation. And yet it stood in the middle of a district crowded with rundown businesses, noisy market traders, workaday printing works, vulgar pubs, slums and brothels. Her Majesty had objected to the blue lamps outside the Bow Street police station in front of the theatre. She had decreed that these beacons of law and order criminalised the atmosphere in which Society liked to convene and had commanded that their blue glass be removed. She really did not appreciate that if ever there was a building that required the near proximity of police protection the Royal Italian Opera House was that building.

I had never been inside before. Its Bow Street facade, despite the enormity of the columns and portico above the carriage entrance, was strangely self-effacing. This was because the road was comparatively narrow and flanked by the imposing court rooms and police station opposite. There was no space to get far enough away to take in the front of the famous theatre in a single, awestruck gaze. It was as if the bastion of privilege wished not to attract the admiring glances that would turn to envy.

To my untutored eyes walking into the entrance hall was what I imagined walking into Buckingham Palace must be like. I was agog at the plush magnificence of everything. A single dark red carpet poured down the Grand Staircase like a river of blood and filled the expanse of the foyer at street level. Gold filigree lamp brackets snaked out of the walls between the statues in their niches. The woodwork of the heavy doors that led down to the orchestra stalls gleamed like the darkest treacle.

'This is nothing,' Father Grantley murmured with a *blasé* smile. 'Wait until we get upstairs.'

It was just over a week into the New Year and I had successfully played for two Sundays at St. Paul's Church. The management of the Opera House had still not responded to my request for an interview, but its proposed subject, the late Signor Baritoni, had nevertheless communicated strangely from beyond the grave. A bewigged footman in a scarlet and gold frock coat had delivered a letter from the theatre housekeeper to Father Grantley. Apparently the clock in the Retiring Room behind the Royal Box had stopped and was suspected of needing repair. In consideration of a donation to St. Paul's, would the clergyman consider examining it? Two weeks before his death Mr Baritoni had spoken highly of Mr Grantley's expertise with timepieces and had recommended that he be consulted should the House find itself in need. It was thought that the clock might have to be removed to either the church or the rectory and that, if so, it would take two men to carry it away in its packing case. I was the second porter, in attendance during my lunch hour.

'Would you follow me, please, gentlemen?'

The request was politely uttered by the bewigged footman in a scarlet and gold frock coat, who gave a little bow and led the way up the Grand Staircase. As we ascended, the ceiling became higher and full-length portraits of princes and monarchs adorned the walls. We turned at the first landing and climbed again until we entered what my companion blithely referred to as the "Crush Room". He said the words as if it was a snuggery in a pub, but in fact it was a chamber into which my brother's house in Battersea would have fitted twice over. A line of crystal chandeliers ten feet tall stretched into the distance, an illusion created by the most enormous mirror I had ever seen. It was flanked by two columns, the space between which begged the question 'Where are the thrones?' Huge potted palms rose up in each corner; gilt-encrusted garlands decorated the wall panels of cream stucco that flaunted further portraits of ineffable grandeur. The rich pile of the blood-red carpet seemed bottomless in its reassurance that here, in this palatial haven, the rulers of the world were safe and secure.

Father Grantley bid me stop a moment and the footman waited patiently. The clergyman seemed lost in a reverie of reminiscence. 'I came here two years ago with the Outhwaites for a performance of *Don Giovanni*,' he said sadly. 'Signor Baritoni welcomed us all like a prince of the blood. He stood in this room, right here, and was absolutely at home among the archdukes and duchesses in the audience. He knew everyone by name but always addressed them quite correctly, in friendly yet respectful fashion. Foreign dignitaries he conversed with in German, French or Italian. If a patron could not speak English but only a language that Baritoni didn't speak himself, one of his team of interpreters would be on hand to assist. He studied the names of important members of the audience every morning and would contact the embassies accordingly so that a junior diplomat of the relevant nationality would be here in the evening. What a wonderful man! How will the House get on without him?'

'We don't know, I'm sure, Reverend,' the footman offered diffidently. 'We're all at sea. No one here enjoyed their Christmas.'

We all stood silent for a moment. The great room suddenly seemed empty of meaning.

'Maybe your clock stopped in sympathy,' said Father Grantley gently. 'Come along, we must do what we can to revive the spirit of the House.'

So we resumed our journey, out of the exit at the far end of the Crush Room and into the back of the Grand Tier of the auditorium. From here the view of the stage was perfect: the house curtain a great cliff of red velvet trimmed with gold brocade and the Royal insignia; the lofty proscenium arch of gilded candy-twist pillars; the golden-pink canopy displaying the silhouette of the young Queen. We walked along a corridor behind the right-hand row of boxes, through a discreet door at the end and found ourselves on the landing of an elegant stairwell decorated in the Regency style. Its staircase was not as imposing as the one we had ascended, but was quite grand nevertheless. This, we were informed, was the private entrance for the Royal Family, with its own hallway and entrance from Floral Street, which ran along the north side of the building. Off this landing led a pair of double doors which the footman opened to reveal the Retiring Room.

Ahead of us stretched a mahogany dining table capable of seating ten people. Above it twinkled a cut-glass chandelier and above that arched the pale-blue-and-pink spangled ceiling. To our left were the doors to the Royal Box and to our right a tall, heavily curtained window looked down onto the roof of the porch above the entrance from Floral Street. What captured our attention, however, beyond the long table, was the clock we had come to collect. It sat on a white mantelpiece which boasted the royal coat of arms. Here was a timepiece looking as if it belonged in the era of

Louis XVI, in a casing of ormolu and brown marble. Father Grantley approached it with a look of wonder and longing.

'My word,' he gasped. 'I do believe it's by Raingo Frères. I've seen one rather like it at Syon House.'

'Please don't touch it, sir,' said the footman. 'It's just been polished. The housekeeper insisted we all wear gloves. I have yours here.'

He produced two pairs of white mittens from his pockets and gave them to us. While we put them on he opened a concealed door to the left of the fireplace which revealed a magnificently appointed lavatory. Out of it he fetched the wooden crate in which the clock would travel. Seeing my look of amazement at this sudden revelation of royal fallibility the footman laughed.

'Yes,' he whispered,' they *are* made of flesh and blood.' It was easy to forget amidst such oppressive splendour.

The clock was immensely heavy, but between us Father Grantley and I managed to lift it down into its crate. Once all the rags and paper had been arranged around it as cushioning, the footman produced a receipt and pen.

'Would you sign for it, please, Reverend?'

'We shall take it to the church, I think, Mr Maitheson. If it goes to the rectory I shall come to covet it.' Then Father Grantley turned to the footman: 'To repair this wonderful instrument will be the greatest honour – if I can achieve it. Please inform the housekeeper that she may expect it back in about a fortnight, perhaps a little longer. It will be kept under lock and key at St. Paul's until then.'

Our regal guide bowed yet again and took the document that the vicar had signed. The precious cargo was lifted up and Father Grantley and I had the honour of being allowed to leave the building by the Royal Staircase and out of Her Majesty's private door into Floral Street. As we made our way along that narrow thoroughfare to the church we soon mingled with the workmen and painters by the Opera House's scenery door, then with the camp followers and musicians smoking outside the Artists' Entrance and then with the everyday tradesmen and passers-by of Covent Garden.

15

January 10th, 1891

Dear Miss Mai—

This was all I got to read before the tap-tap at the door told me that Mrs Jones was about to appear. On this occasion she didn't enter the office but only thrust in her scowl to say 'Visitor, Mr Maitheson – outside', before vanishing.

My heart leaped. Could it be Adriana come to call? The thoughts that had racked my brain since her letter had been agony. My faith was certainly proving hard to rouse from its slumbers. However, I knew that if anything terrible had happened, such as her engagement to a gilded youth of the aristocracy or her being attacked by Fenians, the tom-toms of Society gossip would have deafened me.

'Dear Mr Maitheson,' unfamiliar words spoken by a familiar voice greeted me in *The Gentlewoman*'s entrance hall as I beheld the Lady Eleanor Manverham, my employer at Rockbridge Hall. Guilt overcame me as I remembered that I had never answered her letter before Christmas, but I was glad to see her. She looked as fashionable as ever, her honey-yellow hair dressed in what I was sure was the latest style, her pale blue eyes smiling with kindness and sympathy.

'Lady Eleanor,' I said, 'how very, very nice to see you again. I'm so sorry I never replied to your kind letter.'

'Please, Mr Maitheson, you must not worry about that. I do appreciate that the past year has been a time of very great change in your life. It is so easy to become preoccupied with just one's own concerns at such a time.'

I was conscious of her appraising my appearance with great interest and I was about to enquire after her well-being when she continued graciously: 'May I say how very well you are looking and how handsome you appear in that suit?'

'You're very kind, my lady. My new life here does "suit" me – so to speak – and again I am so sorry not to have thanked you for helping me to the situation, but it only became official at the start of the year.'

'That's quite all right, Mr Maitheson. I am so pleased to hear of your progress from Lady Outhwaite. You have done me proud, as I knew you would.'

'Are you here for the Committee Meeting? Of The Maidens of Mercy?'

'I am indeed – and I believe you are required also. We have never had a meeting here before, but in the circumstances it seemed the most convenient place. I think we are gathering in the Boardroom. Would you show me the way?'

I was only too pleased to oblige, happy that the Boardroom today could hold no terrors with Lady Eleanor present.

*

Present also at the meeting in addition to Lady Eleanor (Patron) were Lady Outhwaite (President), Father Grantley (Covent Garden Branch Secretary) and two gentlemen whom I had not met before. They were the charity's medical consultant, Doctor Selhurst, and Treasurer, Mr Mason. These worthies sat around the Boardroom table with their ladyships at either end. As an invited observer I sat at the editor's side table.

Lady Outhwaite opened the proceedings: 'Thank you for coming today, Lady Eleanor and gentlemen. I hope you find the *venue* convenient. It seemed fitting because the purpose of this meeting is to discuss arrangements for a local event, the Royal Gala at the Opera House on the twelfth of next month. I am aware, of course, that this occasion has been in our diaries for some time. However, it was only in early December that H.R.H. gave his gracious consent to be present. It was thought best not to publicise the event until after Christmas so as not to overshadow the Carol Concert, but unfortunately the Carol Concert has come to overshadow it. After that tragic evening Father Grantley had the excellent idea of suggesting that the opera gala also be in memory of Signor Baritoni, to benefit jointly his bereaved family as well as our charity. I am now pleased to inform the Committee that Marlborough House has enthusiastically agreed to this – as have, naturally, the management of the Opera House.'

'That is excellent news, Margarita,' said Father Grantley happily. 'It would have looked so callous for it to be otherwise.' There were sympathetic nods and murmurs of 'Hear, hear' from around the table. I tried to look as if I had never known a thing about the proposal.

'However,' Lady Outhwaite continued, 'in addition to this welcome news, some other matters have arisen … requiring tact and delicacy.'

I saw Lady Eleanor look at me as if to ask whether 'tact and delicacy' were qualities I had ever known Lady Outhwaite to possess, but perhaps the events of the Carol Concert had brought about a Pauline conversion.

'The first of these,' said the President, 'is that Mr Baritoni's death is still the subject of a police investigation. Consequently, and you may rest assured that I have tried every avenue of enquiry I know, and they are many – not a single piece of information relating to the poor gentleman has been vouchsafed, either by Scotland Yard or the Opera House.'

'Forgive me, Margarita,' Father Grantley cut in, 'but do we know if Mr Baritoni's body has been released for burial?'

'We do not even know that, Giles,' Lady Outhwaite replied gravely. 'It is quite infuriating. I dislike paradoxes of any kind. They are often affected and sometimes convincing, but the fact is that Mr Baritoni's death must be the most public and at the same time the most secret in London.'

'It is probable, Margarita,' said Lady Eleanor gently, 'that his family do not wish to be disturbed by enquiries in their time of grief. And do they not, in any case, live in Italy?'

'I believe so, Lady Eleanor,' said the vicar, 'but anyone who has an address for them won't divulge it. I've made some enquiries myself, of course. It seemed incumbent on me to write to them, but I have drawn a blank.'

I ventured to contribute to the discussion: 'If I may, ladies and gentlemen; my own efforts to find out a little more than what Father Grantley has told me of Mr Baritoni have also proved unsuccessful. I don't know how I am to write an obituary of him for the magazine.'

'Yes, Mr Maitheson,' said Lady Outhwaite, 'I was coming to that, in so far as it concerns the matter in hand. I think that when, or if, we do have sufficient material for an obituary, it should await publication until nearer the time of the gala – and perhaps appear only in the printed programme for the evening and not in the magazine at all. In which case, you may still write the piece.'

'Very good, my lady.'

'And as far as your contribution is concerned, Mr Maitheson, and the reason you have been invited to this meeting, is that I hope I may count on you to assist with other editorial matters where the programme is concerned?'

'Of course, my lady.'

'Thank you, Mr Maitheson. And now,' my employer announced, 'we come to the second delicate matter. This arose in my original communication with Marlborough House as well as with Augustus Harris. His Royal Highness will be attending the performance unaccompanied, by which I mean that the Princess of Wales will not be with him.'

A silence heavy with sophisticated understanding greeted this news. Lips were pursed and meaningful glances were exchanged. Even I was aware of the thoughts being entertained around the table. The Prince of Wales' *penchant* for affairs outside of his marriage was pretty widely known. There had been a difference of opinion somewhere. The Princess Alexandra's devotion to charitable causes was celebrated. So why was she not attending this worthy, glittering event?

Lady Outhwaite allowed the speculation to foment in the minds of her audience for just the right amount of time before triumphantly staking her claim to sacred knowledge, that of the Wales' inner circle. 'It is not what you think,' she pronounced with self-satisfaction. 'Her Royal Highness dislikes the opera intensely. She saw it in Paris and refuses to watch it again.'

'Oh, is that all?' Lady Eleanor parried skilfully. 'What is the opera to be given?'

'One of the Prince's favourites,' Lady Outhwaite responded nonchalantly, as if it was common knowledge that Lady Eleanor should have known. '*Philémon et Baucis* by Gounod.'

There were blank faces and mutters of 'Never heard of it' from the Committee, so the President went on to explain: 'It concerns the failure of Jupiter to discover rectitude amongst the peoples of the Earth, so he punishes them by fire. There's a ballet depicting the Orgy of the Phrygians in the second act.'

'Ah,' said Father Grantley. 'That explains everything.'

'But this is hardly suitable fare for a charity such as ours,' Lady Eleanor protested.

'Dear Eleanor,' said Lady Outhwaite crisply, 'it was that opera or no Prince of Wales. Let us embrace Truth: Society depends on hypocrisy in order to function smoothly. The pressing question for us to consider is who shall sit in the Royal Box with H.R.H. He has graciously suggested that it should be you and I and Father Grantley, which I think honours the charity perfectly.'

As the Prince's suggestion was tantamount to a royal command, the matter was settled without demur.

'And so we come to the programme for the evening,' Lady Outhwaite continued, extracting another letter from her portfolio. 'We have no say in this. It has been drawn up by Marlborough House and Augustus Harris. I will have copies posted to you, but it is as follows: 7.50 pm. The audience to have taken seats. Arrival of H.R.H. at the Royal entrance. H.R.H. to be presented to special guests in the Retiring Room. Presentation of Mr Baritoni's immediate family by Augustus Harris; 8 pm. H.R.H. and guests enter Royal Box. National Anthem; 8.03 pm. Overture and Act One; 8.44 pm. Interval and Reception in the Retiring Room; 9.14 pm. Act Two; 10.15 pm. Reception in the Retiring Room. Presentation of selected Unfortunates to H.R.H.; 10.50 pm. Departure of H.R.H.; 11.00pm. Carriages.'

'"Selected Unfortunates"?' wondered Lady Eleanor. 'Who are they?'

'H.R.H.'s request,' came the answer. 'He expressly asked to meet two or three women whom the Maidens of Mercy have assisted. I suggest that Father Grantley recruits them from this area, that Doctor Selhurst ensures they are in good health and that the charity sees to it that they are clean and presentable. Giles, dear, we need women who have fallen, but who with our help have helped themselves and risen up out of the mire.'

'I quite understand,' said Father Grantley. 'Leave it to me, Margarita. I shall make enquiries. If the worst comes to the worst, we could always enlist Mrs Jones.'

16

It wasn't a dream. I was wearing white tie and tails, immaculate and perfectly fitting. My patent leather dress shoes gleamed reassuringly, as did my hair slicked down with subtly scented oil from Penhaligon's. I felt like Cinderella being allowed to go to the ball, which in this version of the story was the Royal Gala at the Opera House on February 12, 1891. Moreover, I was not climbing the endless side stairs to "the Gods" but the Grand Staircase to the Crush Room.

The fairy godmother who had made this possible was Lady Eleanor. When it transpired that the Baritoni family would not be travelling to London to attend the Gala, the box next door to the royal one had become vacant and had been taken over by the Cormanstons, who had moved along the line to be nearer the Prince of Wales. What had been their box was then free to accommodate what Lady Outhwaite referred to as 'the chosen few': Lady Lambe-Weston, *The Gentlewoman*'s music critic; Mr and Mrs Wilkins and, at Lady Eleanor's insistence, myself.

It wasn't a dream. There before me in the Crush Room was Adriana, whom I had not seen or heard from since her letter. And I had never seen her look so lovely. She was the picture of the fairytale princess in a pale blue gown and diamond-and-sapphire tiara. She made it very clear to me how happy she was to see me by the way she smiled. I knew that all was well between us and I felt no hesitation in approaching her party to make polite enquiries of the family and to be introduced at last to Viscount Cormanston.

'Can't say this opera is my idea of entertainment,' he opined gruffly, 'but it is vital we show ourselves united with H.R.H. Don't you agree, Mr Maitheson?'

'Wholeheartedly, my lord. The show must go on at all times.'

Adriana's father was a tall, bluff, square-shouldered military man. He must have been about fifty years old, with distinguished-looking silver hair and a sunburnt complexion. His demeanour celebrated absolutism in all its forms. His brown-eyed gaze was unwavering.

'You're going to write about this shindig for *The Gentlewoman*, I suppose?'

'Yes, my lord – if I'm allowed to.'

Lord Cormanston gave a little smile of understanding. He and I obviously shared an opinion of Lady Outhwaite but he was not a man to allow disloyalty in the ranks: 'Damn capable woman, Margarita. She'll end up Prime Minister if we're not careful, what? Well now, so nice to have made your acquaintance, Mr Maitheson, but will you excuse me? I need to have a word with William Devonshire over there.'

So I was left to converse with mother and daughter, who asked if I had been to the Opera House before. I told them about my two recent visits with Father Grantley, when I had helped him with the Retiring Room clock. The monumental timepiece had been sitting in the vestry of St. Paul's Church for nearly four weeks. Every Sunday morning before the service Father Grantley would give me a report on its labyrinthine workings. The catalogue of its shortcomings was endless. It had not been well maintained and was seldom used. Its mechanism had never once been cleaned in thirty years … but the clergyman had been happy in his hobby, dismantling and polishing each tiny part and then reassembling the whole. It was clear that he had been obsessed with the project, as if he could in a sense bring his friend Signor Baritoni back to life by restoring this little part of the Opera House. To have it working again in time for the Royal Gala had become a matter of honour.

Eventually the day came when I was summoned to help carry the clock back to its place on the marble mantel piece, when our efforts were supervised once again by the bewigged footman in scarlet and gold.

'And is it working now?' Adriana asked.

'As far as I know. We'll soon see, won't we?' I replied proudly, for I too had been invited to the Retiring Room to be presented to His Royal Highness on arrival.

*

The rest of the audience had been seated, but we were in the corridor behind our boxes, waiting to be summoned into the royal presence. I was nervous. Reports that the Prince could put anyone at ease seemed to refer to another world to which I did not belong. Then I heard the aforementioned footman requesting us to follow him and one by one we were announced as we entered the Retiring Room.

Lady Outhwaite went in first so that she could present us all and I was last to go in. The room was very full of people. The dining table had been removed and three smaller tables had been set up in the corners from which refreshments would be served later: tiny, delicate sandwiches; oysters; ices and champagne. I could barely see His Royal Highness through the little crowd. I glimpsed the footman next to the Prince, standing beside the fireplace and then I was standing before the familiar, grey bearded gentlemen who puffed on a half-smoked cigar and smiled graciously. Close to, he was an enormous, all-embracing presence, a Father Christmas in black and white, with a blue sash and sparkling star. Because the image of this man was engrained on the popular consciousness, the reality was not at all intimidating.

'How do you do, Mr Maitheson?'

'Your Royal Highness.' I bowed correctly from the neck up and shook the proffered hand.

The thick, velvety, Teutonic-toned voice spoke again: 'Lady Outhwaite informs me that you are the *fraulein* fount of wisdom at *The Gentlewoman.*'

I laughed nervously and answered: 'Yes, Sir. I am the "Miss Maitheson" of the "Letters" page.'

'I wish my Mama would write to you for advice, Mr Maitheson. I am sure you would counsel her better than most of the people she listens to.'

There was a happy ripple of laughter around the room.

'You do me too much honour, Sir.' I bowed again.

'Not at all. And now, is it time for the overture?' He turned round to consult the magnificent clock behind him. It was ticking away confidently. Its minute hand hovered a fraction of an inch before the 12 and a faint whirring from within the marble casing told us that the chimes of eight were about to sound.

I shall never forget the roar of applause as the Prince entered the box and the entire audience rose for the National Anthem. The orchestra played it magnificently and the rows of figures in black, white, scarlet, gold, silver and every soft, silky pastel shade swam before my eyes. Twinkling jewellery; bristling whiskers; crisply starched linen; beautiful shoulders; enveloping bosoms; proud faces – these people were completely oblivious to the hardships of the world only a couple of hundred yards away. And yet, despite the dichotomy, I found this display moving because it was heartfelt. This audience had prayed for it. They believed absolutely in the values that this occasion celebrated, values that some of them had fought for and for which many were prepared to die.

*

'Oh no, not nearly as good as *Faust* …'

'Well, I'm glad we're not eating what poor old Jupiter was offered …'

'We stayed at Belvoir two weeks ago.'

'Hunting all right?'

'Splendid. Johnny Rutland was in very good form.'

'I don't think William will ever get over Freddy's murder.'

'And who shall I be meeting after the second act?'

'Let me consult, Sir. Father Grantley?'

'Ah yes, Your Royal Highness, there will be three ladies: a Mrs Jones, who now works for Lady Outhwaite at the magazine; a Sally Jardine, who lives at St Agnes' Mission off Drury Lane – she's a new recruit who is fighting the demon drink and making wonderful progress; and a young woman from Seven Dials called Jenny Crampton who is learning to be a typist.'

The champagne and sandwiches had fuelled great cheerfulness in the Retiring Room during the interval, though it was frustrating being obliged to communicate with Adriana through looks only.

Lady Eleanor had blanched slightly at the mention of Sally Jardine. 'Mr Maitheson,' she whispered, 'please don't tell me that old Nanny Selkirk is here tonight. I had no idea that she'd applied to The Maidens for assistance.'

I was about to relate my encounter with the old woman before Christmas when Father Grantley suddenly exclaimed: 'Oh no! I'm so sorry, everyone. Your Royal Highness, I'm so very sorry. The Raingo Frères appears to have stopped – and after all my work.'

Lady Outhwaite cut in smoothly: 'Don't worry, Giles. No one will notice. We still have twenty minutes of the interval. I'm sure they'll get it going again during Act Two.'

'Allow me, dear lady,' the Prince of Wales offered. 'There's a trick I learned from the clock keeper at Sandringham.' His Royal Highness stepped towards the fire and reached out towards the timepiece, but Father Grantley stayed his hand.

'Please don't touch it, Sir,' said the clergyman. 'I do apologise for my impertinence, but this machine is in delicate health. Permit me to demonstrate a little trick of my own.'

The Prince conceded gracefully and the room fell silent as everyone watched Father Grantley who with quick, neat movements swung open the glass face cover on its hinges. Immediately, between finger and thumb, he took the point of the minute hand, which stood at five minutes to nine, and moved it forward by five minutes, then back; then forward ten minutes and back; then forward fifteen minutes and back. He then closed the glass front. Now the whole room held its breath … before clapping with delight as the ticking resumed.

'You are a master, Reverend,' said the Prince admiringly. 'I congratulate you. Let us all have some more champagne.'

Father Grantley bowed and smiled. 'Thank you, Sir,' he said. 'It would have been too embarrassing to have failed in your presence. It doesn't always work, but I've found that with the Raingo Frères pieces it usually does.'

'Very good to know, Reverend. I believe we have fifteen of them at Marlborough House.'

Now conversation started again, but I was aware of a change of atmosphere in the room. The Cormanstons and the servants all stiffened in their demeanour and were silent. It was as if they were waiting for a signal or command. Sure enough the Prince said: 'Lady Outhwaite, we have had a new Retiring Room built just below this one, specifically for the ladies when gentlemen wish to smoke. But we cannot decide on the *décor*. I should so welcome your advice. I wonder whether you and the other ladies would care to look at it?'

'But of course, Sir. We should be honoured. Will your man here show us the way?'

All the ladies curtseyed and the bewigged footman in scarlet and gold bowed and went forth at the head of a feminine exodus. Then the waiters followed so that only the gentlemen were left behind with His Royal Highness. There was a pause whilst we waited for the Prince to restart the conversation or perhaps invite us to smoke. We heard the ladies descending the Royal Staircase and a few seconds of silence passed when I was acutely conscious of the ticking of the clock.

17

The whistle pierced the air like a banshee. It came from below and was immediately repeated outside in Floral Street, then all along the street in both directions. From behind the double doors into the Royal Box I heard another blast and the commands of what sounded like police constables. There was a whoosh, then a sudden grinding and groaning of iron as the fire curtain over the stage began to descend. Far away I heard a bell and running footsteps from the Bow Street end of Floral Street, all mixed with the growing cries and remonstrations of members of the audience as they were ordered to leave the theatre. At the same time the concealed door to the royal lavatory swung open and a bearded man in grey tweed came forward and pushed Father Grantley into the centre of the room, then down onto the floor. A revolver appeared and was clapped to the clergyman's head. It was shocking to see the vicar treated so violently. Mr Wilkins and I looked at each other in astonishment until Lord Cormanston shouted 'We must leave, Sir, now,' and pulled the Prince towards the staircase. 'You two, Maitheson, Wilkins, follow us.'

Amidst the rapidly mounting din of shouts and screams everywhere I heard the following spoken very rapidly by the man with the gun: 'Giles Patrick Grantley, I am Colonel Ford of Her Majesty's Inspectorate of Explosives. You are under arrest for the attempted assassination of The Prince of Wales and of the Viscount Cormanston and the attempted murder of all those persons present. You do not have to say anything, but anything you do say may be used in evidence against you.'

Grantley's face tightened with fury. His eyes quivered with tiny movements as if seeking a solution or an escape route. Then he looked at me and said: 'I am sorry you have to witness this charade, Richard, and even sorrier you keep company with tyrants, flatterers and hypocrites. I really meant *you* no harm at all. You'd better run, hadn't you?'

I couldn't look at him. I couldn't believe he had cold-bloodedly built an infernal machine that was set to explode. Was it true? And had he murdered others with such devices?

'You heard the man,' the colonel barked. 'Get out now.'

I looked behind me and saw that I was alone with these two.

'We'll leave when we're ready, don't worry,' the colonel continued. 'Captain leaves a sinking ship last. Go. That is an *order* in the name of the Queen.'

I saw the minute hand of the clock behind him edge forward and I ran. Thank God I had twice before been shown this way out or I might have panicked at the bottom of the Royal Staircase. A police constable was by the exit into Floral Street, lantern in hand.

'Any more up there, sir?'

'Just two. They're on the way.'

'That way, sir. Don't go down Hanover Place. We're hoping the blast will funnel down that alley. Don't wait, sir.'

As I started running towards the Bow Street corner, I thought I heard a gunshot behind me, but I didn't stop to look round. After the bright lights of the theatre and all its chandeliers, Floral Street seemed a chasm of darkness. The white wall of the Opera House reared up like a cliff to my right. Ahead of me, behind a line of lanterns, a crowd of people were being pushed back by a row of constables. Members of the audience were pouring out of the Gods' entrance. A few doors slammed on my left as people left the warehouses and workshops. In front of the human barrier of policemen stood the Prince of Wales and Lord Cormanston. A sergeant with a megaphone in one hand and a stopwatch in the other stood next to them.

'Six minutes,' he bellowed.

Then, above the cries and the alarm bell ringing in the police station opposite, I heard the wailing of a very familiar voice: 'Mr Maitheson, help.'

High above me, leaning out of a window about forty feet up, was Mrs Jones.

'I'm stuck in the lavatory, Mr Maitheson. The door's jammed.'

'Ladders,' I yelled, looking over the crowd. 'What about that fire engine? Does that have ladders?'

'Nothing comes through, young man, until after the blast,' shouted the sergeant, before muttering, 'and there'd better be a blast after all this.'

'Don't move, Mrs Jones. Stay there where we can see you,' and with that I started running back down Floral Street towards the constable at the Royal Entrance. A roar of 'Come back, man, you're mad' followed me as I nearly collided with Colonel Ford running out of the exit I had just left.

'That's it, constable,' he ordered. 'You must pull out now. What are you doing, Maitheson? Pull out, I say.'

'There's a woman trapped up there, Colonel,' I panted. 'Please come with me to the scenery door. There may be a ladder inside. Please.'

Ford looked at his watch. 'All right, man, but we are going to run like hell. Constable, follow us.'

'Four minutes. Stand by to withdraw.'

Ahead in James Street was another line of lanterns held by policemen pushing back the onlookers. Some of these were in the costumes of Ancient Greece, dancers waiting to perform the Orgy of the Phrygians. As they screamed at us to turn back, my mind shut down into a cold steel tunnel of purpose. Scenery door. Locked? No. It slid open to reveal a cavern of pitch darkness. All lights shut down inside.

'Shine your lantern round, man.'

The ghostly pool revealed boxes, rows of ropes, looming canvas flats, chairs and music stands. No ladders.

'All men to pull out now,' came voices from two different megaphones. 'All men to pull out now.'

'That's it, Maitheson,' gasped the colonel. 'I'm sorry.'

'No,' I cried, 'look there. It's a mattress.' And there was, but it was huge, about ten feet square and very deep.

It took the three of us to haul the monster out of its corner to the door. We all tore off our jackets. I was completely drenched. I had never felt so wet since my night in the Thames. Pull. Grunt. Shove. Pull. Grunt. Nearly there. Nearly there. Out on the street now.

'We'll never get it up there in time,' the constable sobbed.

'Yes,' I shouted – and then I saw the little truck on its side, up against the wall just inside the scenery door. I ran to it, pulled it down savagely and pushed it outside.

And how we heaved to get the unwieldly mass of canvas and feathers on top of the little cart. 'Here, sir. With me on this side. Hold it steady, Constable. Don't let it fall off.'

'Don't leave me, Mr Maitheson,' screamed Mrs Jones. 'Dear Mr Maitheson, please don't leave me.'

'Two constables to help those men,' roared the sergeant. 'You and you, go.'

Twenty seconds later the great wobbling square was under the window.

'You must jump, Mrs Jones.'

'I can't ... I can't. It's too far down.'

Then the whistles again. 'All men pull back. All men pull *back*.'

Ford and the constables ran to the line of lanterns which had started to move backwards across Bow Street. The wall of officers had joined arms and were forcing the crowds away, away from the mighty edifice that towered above them. But I stayed with the mattress.

'Mrs Jones,' I pleaded, 'you must jump – *now*.'

18

Through the sergeant's megaphone came the imperious tones of Lady Outhwaite: 'If you don't jump, Jones, I will send you back to Middlesbrough.'

'No, my lady.'

'Then jump.'

Just as the little figure sailed out into the cold night air and plummeted to the mattress, thirty yards away the explosion tore through the side of the building. I flung myself on top of the woman in front of me. There was a rumbling and crumbling of masonry. A maelstrom of glass, splinters and shreds of fabric swept over us. Dust, and more dust and still more dust enveloped us. The whole of Covent Garden seemed to be screaming. Vainly did the stentorian sergeant call for quiet so as to give his commands, but Colonel Ford knew a trick or two of that and fired twice into the air, which brought the crowds to order.

'Get back there,' he shouted, 'and let the doctors through. And two ambulances. Move aside there. Mr Maitheson, can you hear me?'

'Yes, sir,' I choked hoarsely.

'Good man. We're coming to fetch you. Don't move. Mrs Jones?'

Beneath me I could feel a quivering movement. Mrs Jones was whimpering: 'No, not Middlesbrough, not Middlesbrough.'

'She's alive, colonel, that's all I know.'

I felt cuts from the glass on the back of my hands and back, but I was not bleeding profusely. I moved a little and looked along the street. The constable had been right: the full force of the explosion had blown into Hanover Place, which had limited the damage at either end of Floral Street. But the implications of horror began to sink in. Anyone in the Retiring Room would have been killed. As it was, only fragments of Father Grantley would be found, for I presumed that the shot I had heard earlier had marked his end.

Now the doctors had reached us. I recognised one of them. He was the anonymous Samaritan from the Carol Concert and he led me to an ambulance in Bow Street. The other doctor carried Mrs Jones, who was in profound shock but who did not appear to be otherwise injured. No bones broken, it was thought, and no heart attack. The memory of her experiences in that terrible town had been her greatest trauma. She was taken at once to Charing Cross Hospital and to her credit, and to my utter amazement, Lady Outhwaite went with her in the ambulance.

Policemen had started to move the crowds down towards the Strand and a detachment of officers began erecting a barricade around the front of the theatre. The fire brigade had moved in to combat the fires. By dint of a great deal of shouting and whinnying a line of carriages had manoeuvred themselves in front of the police station alongside the second ambulance where I was having my cuts dressed. Waiting on the pavement to greet me as I emerged bandaged and blanketed was a shivering group of Prince, patrons and patronesses. No one had had time to retrieve their coats or cloaks.

Adriana rushed up and hugged me. She was weeping. 'I'm sorry,' she said, 'I'm so sorry. Are you all right?'

Then her father approached me and shook me by the hand, notwithstanding its bandaged state. 'We are all going to Cormanston House,' he said,' well, not the Wilkinses and Lady Lambe-Weston – they want to go home – but everyone else, for some supper and much-needed whisky. Would you honour us by coming too? You can travel in our carriage and please don't worry about dress – you are welcome to borrow some clothes of my son.'

I accepted gratefully and we were all on the point of embarking when we heard the singing: 'I know that my Redeemer liveth, and that he shall stand at the latter day upon the Earth.' It was faint, in a quavering soprano with a lilt of the Highlands of Scotland.

'Your Royal Highness?' she called.

'Yes, madam?'

'Your Royal Highness,' said the woman coming out of the gloom, 'I am Sally Jardine and Father Grantley said you wanted to meet me.'

She was clean. Her hair was properly dressed. She wore a little make-up and her gown was fresh under a fur-trimmed top coat. She was fragrant, or at least as far as I could tell at a distance of twenty feet and, judging by her gait, she was sober.

The Prince looked to Lady Eleanor for guidance and she came forward to make the introduction, amazed at seeing her former governess in a new guise.

Miss Jardine was calm and smiled serenely. 'I have seen a Great Light, Your Royal Highness,' she announced, 'and I want you to see it also. "For shall not the earth become as white as the new-born lamb when it is cleansed of Sin?"'

And in that moment the scales fell from my eyes. I remembered that Father Grantley before Christmas had said to the woman that the "fat folks of Babylon shall perish in the flames and at thine own hand." Here was the anaconda that I had glimpsed in the murky waters of my memory and now it showed its head. It took the form of a human being, unhinged and dispossessed, manipulated and indoctrinated so as to become a living, breathing infernal machine.

Instinctively I backed away very slowly. There was only one person who could help us. I turned, saw him and went to him quickly. 'Colonel,' I whispered. 'I know that woman and I sense she is carrying a bomb to kill the Prince. She was a follower of Father Grantley's and she is not sane.'

The soldier looked into my eyes, saw the truth, raised his revolver, took aim and fired. Never had I seen such steely resolution. I did nothing to stop him because I knew I was right. If I had had a gun and my hand had not been bandaged I would have fired the shot myself. She never saw it coming. She was killed instantly.

'Catch her, Sir,' cried the colonel. 'Don't let her fall. Lower her very gently.' And His Royal Highness had done it the instant the shot was fired, springing forward like a tiger and holding the woman under the arms, keeping his body away from hers and then slowly, very slowly laying her out on the pavement.

A shocked silence descended on Bow Street and once again Colonel Ford gave commands: 'Everyone move away. Very carefully. Do not touch that body. Sergeant, get your men to evacuate anyone left in this area to a radius of one hundred yards from this corpse – including everyone in the station. Those going to Cormanston House should go now. I will join you there shortly.'

Meekly and without a word we did as we were ordered. One by one the ambulance and the carriages pulled away and headed north to Long Acre and Lincoln's Inn Fields.

*

I was changing into some clean clothes that had been brought to the bathroom by Lord Cormanston's valet. They were a little too big, but that was better than entering the dining-room in the bloody, bedraggled state I had been in. The man was tying my tie when I heard a boom from the direction of Covent Garden and I knew what it was. Colonel Ford had judged it safer to detonate Miss Jardine's body *in situ*.

As I entered the dining-room the conversation stopped, my host rose from his chair at one end of the table and so too, to my surprise, did the Prince of Wales. I was shown to my seat on the left of Lady Cormanston with His Royal Highness opposite me. Diagonally across the table was Adriana and next to her an empty place. Lady Eleanor sat on my left.

'We won't wait for the colonel,' said Lady Cormanston to the butler. 'Please serve supper now.'

My own food had to be cut up for me by a footman. I think everyone had grown very hungry standing out in the cold and we concentrated on eating and drinking, but gradually I became aware that they couldn't say what they wanted to say because they were waiting for Colonel Ford to arrive. I felt a little as if I was in the Boardroom at *The Gentlewoman* and that I had been summoned by Lady Outhwaite's Tribunal of Transgression. The atmosphere became quite uneasy until eventually Lord Cormanston spoke.

'Mr Maitheson, I gather from Lady Eleanor that you can be utterly depended upon to keep a secret.'

'Indeed, my lord, and I can vouch for Lady Eleanor's discretion in return.'

'Just so, sir,' said my host. 'That is most encouraging. Of course, Lady Eleanor's husband – well, his stock in trade is secrets. The Manverhams Bank would have failed long ago if this dear lady's discretion was not legendary. So what we have here, Mr Maitheson, is a situation where a story is going to be told, probably written by you and first published in *The Gentlewoman*. And we are going to have to decide tonight, we six and Colonel Ford when he gets here, just what that story will be. You and my daughter are familiar with editorial meetings, of course, so it shouldn't be too strange.'

'No, my lord.'

'Well, let me begin by saying,' the viscount continued, 'that we don't need Colonel Ford's presence to compliment you on your magnificent conduct this evening. You have displayed courage, gallantry, initiative and acute intuition that would do honour to the finest officer I can think of.'

'Thank you, my lord. I hardly know what to say.' I had entered a new world. This was a kind of recognition to which I was not used.

His Royal Highness leant a little across the table and said gently: 'Lord Cormanston is right, Mr Maitheson. You have served your country bravely without a thought for yourself.'

It would have been impolite in the extreme to disagree with the Prince of Wales, but the truth was that I had done some of it for myself. The person who had given me the spur to enter this new world was sitting across the table. I knew that if I did not speak privately to Adriana before leaving this house tonight then all was lost.

'You are too kind, Sir.'

I was saved from further embarrassment by the butler entering and presenting a telegram on a salver to the Prince.

'This has just arrived, Sir, from Windsor.'

'Will you excuse me, Cormanston? Lady Cormanston? You never know, Mama may have decided to call it a day.'

As His Royal Highness opened the envelope, a footman announced Colonel Ford, who entered hastily and apologetically and was shown to his seat at the table.

'Well done, Andrew,' said Lady Cormanston. 'I think you are just in time.'

Suddenly there was a feeling of hilarity in the room. The Prince threw back his head and laughed, took a sip of wine, then proclaimed in a voice that was not his own, in a voice that I had never thought to hear ever again: 'Signor Conte, signore, messeri and signorina, this wire is from His Royal Highness himself and here is what it says: "Bravo, Baritoni, I always knew you would pull it off. Gather your performance was superb. Only regret the Opera House will suffer building works yet again. Gratitude and congratulations, Bertie."'

19

It had been an evening of so many shocks to Lady Eleanor and me that she and I could only stare at one another. Everyone else at the table had concealed the plot for months and only the sad expression on Adriana's face stopped me from feeling angry and used.

Part of the hurt of which I was conscious was the sensation of being so ignorant. It was how I imagined a betrayed husband must feel. It dawned on me that dozens of people had been involved, from the anonymous doctor at the Carol Concert and the musician who had caught Baritoni's body to Augustus Harris and the bewigged footman in scarlet and gold. They had all known what was happening and I had not. If I did not find out everything now the past few months would seem devoid of meaning.

After the initial outbursts of surprise and disbelief – mixed with joy, of course, that Baritoni had never died – some explanations were to be forthcoming. People were clearly eager to explain, so I asked and asked …

'Back in December, Colonel, did you arrange for my brother Arthur to be investigated by Scotland Yard?'

'Yes, Mr Maitheson, I did. His work at the Chelsea Barracks was the reason, mainly. When it was decided that you might be able to help this matter along, it was considered necessary to check your army connections. An ordnance clerk can sometimes gain access to restricted material or information.'

'And how did you think I could help you?' I asked angrily, 'Apart from risking my life, that is? What if I had dropped the clock, lugging it back across Covent Garden?'

'I will soothe with the whisky,' said Lord Cormanston, motioning to the butler to bring me some, 'and please allow me to answer that question, Mr Maitheson. You heard me talk just now about a story to be told, about a suitable narrative of events. The whole aim of this grand design has been to construct a narrative of events that would convict a master murderer in a court of law. Evidence of intent is very difficult to secure.'

'Especially,' the colonel cut in, 'with infernal machines. If the thing goes off, just about every atom of scientific evidence is instantly destroyed.'

'We need you as a witness to just about everything,' Lord Cormanston explained, 'for you may rest assured that we will all be testifying at the enquiry into tonight. We need your evidence more than anyone else's. We needed an unwitting spy whom no one would suspect and the best spy is an innocent spy.'

'Is Grantley really dead?' I asked.

'Oh yes,' Colonel Ford replied grimly.

'Did you shoot him, sir?'

'Yes, I did, but the official version for him will be suicide. We have the evidence, we have the witnesses. You heard what Grantley said on being arrested. And as for Miss Jardine, did you hear the explosion half an hour ago, after you'd got here?'

'We all did,' said Lady Cormanston.

'There will be no court martial over this, young man,' the colonel continued. 'We are at war and war is about taking calculated risks. The most difficult one in this battle was judging the length of the delay that Grantley would set for detonation. He knew that only a device that could be set in plain view of witnesses would look innocent enough and give him a hope of getting out alive.

'From the moment the clock came back from the church it was guarded day and night. Once he had wound it and set it going no one touched it. He could only set the detonator after the Prince had arrived, because H.R.H. may have backed out of the engagement, and only the interval would give Grantley the best chance of leaving unnoticed. Fifteen minutes would give him plenty of room for manoeuvre. But he had to set it in the interval, and to explode in the interval, to ensure H.R.H. being as close as possible to the clock. The detonator setting works rather like the combination lock of a safe: you move the minute hand forward and back in multiples of five minutes. We came across something similar earlier this year that had not exploded.'

'And the code for letting that footman know the number of minutes' delay was the number of Raingo Frères clocks said to be at Marlborough House?' Adriana asked.

'Exactly, Miss Creston. The police and theatre staff had been briefed for scenarios of five, ten, and fifteen or upwards minutes – separate whistle signals for each scenario.'

Now Lady Eleanor asked a question of no one in particular: 'And what would have happened if the machine had exploded unexpectedly, or if your guesses had been wrong?'

Signor Baritoni answered this: 'That would have been unfortunate, my lady, but Father Grantley would still have failed. For the real Prince of Wales was never in the building.'

'Do you make a living on the halls impersonating H.R.H., signor Baritoni?' Lady Eleanor asked.

The gentleman's reply was dignified in the extreme: 'No, my lady, I work for Her Majesty's Secret Service and have done so since coming from Milan, where I was police chief at La Scala. The idea to impersonate the Prince came about when a patron here mistook me for the Prince in the Crush Room. Particularly in evening dress there is a resemblance.

'For this adventure I had nearly two months hidden at Marlborough House to prepare. His clothes were altered a little to fit me and the hair was easy. I simply washed out my own black dye and grew my beard longer. It was his way of speaking that took time to learn.'

'And of course it helped that everyone believed that Mr Baritoni was dead,' I said. 'Colonel Ford, were you the man who fired the blank in the church, and rendered Miss Creston and Mr Wilkins unconscious?'

'I was indeed. A lot of rehearsals we had to get all that right. But Grantley had to see the fake killing happen under his nose.'

'I venture to suggest, Papa, that *The Gentlewoman* should serialise a novella, not just print a news item. How else will the story be done justice?'

Lord Cormanston smiled before replying. 'I am sorry to say, my dear, that the threat we face from murderers of Grantley's ilk is all too serious. As you know. We are at war with these people and the Empire needs to read the unvarnished truth of how this battle was fought and – thank God – won. Mr Maitheson, I wonder if I could have a private word with you in the library?'

'Of course, my lord.'

The room smelled of old leather and paper. The fire had burned low and only one lamp was lit, so that the shelves of volumes towered up into the gloom and the portraits of military-looking ancestors glowered down out of it.

Lord Cormanston bade me take a chair by the fire and then sat opposite me. Now he appeared older and, though comfortable in his own home, somewhat vulnerable. I wondered what the matter was.

'Mr Maitheson,' he said, 'what I wanted to say to you is this. It wouldn't surprise me at all if you took a very dim view of my family and what we stand for and if that is the case I am very sorry. The world of secret agents and state-sponsored assassination is a very sordid one, but you have to understand that it has been a vital part of governing this country for centuries, going back to Sir Francis Walsingham in the time of Elizabeth and even further. Experience of it at first hand when one is young is probably disheartening. I wouldn't blame you if you felt angry with us for using you as a pawn in our game of soldiers and I sincerely hope you will forgive us if that is the case.

'But in particular I hope you will forgive my daughter's part in it all. You see, I know that she is anxious that you do not think ill of her and, indeed, I know she would like to talk to you. So I am going to send her to you now so that you and she may come to an understanding.

'Please stay as long as you like. The carriage will take you home whenever you wish. Help yourself to a drink or a cigarette if you want – you'll find it all over there. And may I just add finally – and I hope you will not think me presumptuous or interfering – that if you should just *happen*, quite on the off chance, to entertain the notion of proposing to my daughter ... either tonight or at some time in the future ... then I want you to know that her mother and I would be very, very happy.'

*

Later that night I was crossing the river in Lord Cormanston's carriage. We were going over Westminster Bridge and over to my left I could see Hungerford Bridge which, months ago one foggy night, I had failed to cross. I had been uncertain and unhappy, drunk and suicidal. My survival had been, as the Duke of Wellington had described Waterloo, "the nearest run thing you ever saw in your life."

It is one thing to have strength of conviction, to be honest with yourself and with others and to accept what you do not want to change. But if you are unsure about what you want or have been too afraid to ask for it, or fight for it, or too weak-willed to work for it, or too poor to facilitate it, then the chances of finding your way through the fog of life's confusions are slim.

Back in the library of Cormanston House Adriana and I had listened to our hearts, spoken openly and fearlessly about our concerns, and had decided that we both knew what we wanted and how to achieve it. The received wisdom, or cynicism, of the world is not necessarily so very helpful. The truth can only be discovered in the individual circumstances of the couple concerned.

A new form of words was going to transform my life in the near future, a phrase that embraced a change that I longed for with all my heart. The phrase was: "Dear *Mrs* Maitheson."

ACKNOWLEDGEMENTS

Dear Miss Maitheson is a work of historical fiction and its characters are entirely fictional, with the obvious exceptions of the named celebrities. One character, however, who really did exist may not be an obvious historical figure. He is Colonel A. Ford of H.M. Inspectorate of Explosives. I don't know what the 'A' stands for, so I have called him Andrew. I read about him in a wonderful book published by Endeavour Press in 2013 called *The Best of the Strand Magazine*. In it there is an essay on the dynamite terrorists of the 1880s and 1890s. Colonel A. Ford was one of the heroes who protected the nation. His appearance, actions and opinions in this story are fictional, however.

Another book that I consulted frequently and found indispensable was *Covent Garden Past* by John Richardson (Historical Publications, 1995): fascinating, splendidly written and beautifully illustrated.

Helen Robinson, managing director of *The Lady* magazine, and Sergiu Canschi, its IT manager, very kindly gave me access to the archives of *The Lady* for 1890 and 1892, for which I am most grateful.

My dear friend Barry Stewart's company, guidance and hospitality at the Royal Opera House in London, and elsewhere, have been a source of support and pleasure for many years. This story could not have happened without him.

As with the prequel to this book, *The Fear at Rockbridge Hall*, a number of friends assisted and encouraged me. My thanks again to: Gail Berry, Stephanie Dawes, Fiona Evans, Dominic Gore-Andrews, Linda Kelly, Sarah-Jane Kitching, Faith Saunders, Kate Titley, Penny Walker and Jonathan Wilkins … as well as to all the team at Endeavour Press, in particular James Faktor and Jasmin Kirkbride.

About the author

Tim Heath was born in London, educated in Sussex and Dorset and read English at University College London. He has been an actor, director and writer all his life, appearing on stage, TV, radio and film (for more information please visit www.timheath1.com). His previous books are: *The Dragons at Marshmouldings* (a children's book); a stage play, *Sherlock Holmes: The Adventure at Sir Arthur Sullivan's* and *The Fear at Rockbridge Hall* (the prequel to *Dear Miss Maitheson* and also published by Endeavour Press). He is unmarried and lives in London.

If you enjoyed *Dear Miss Maitheson*, please share your thoughts on Amazon by leaving a review.

For more free and discounted eBooks every week, sign up to our newsletter.

Follow us on Twitter, Facebook and Instagram.

Printed in Great Britain
by Amazon